LEILA AND NUGGET MYSTERY

COLLECTION #1

BOOK ONE: Who Stole Mr. T?

BOOK TWO: The Case With No Clues

BOOK THREE: Bark at the Park

DESERAE & DUSTIN BRADY

CONTENTS

BOOK 1: Who Stole Mr. T?

1. The Abominable Snow Dog   1
2. Turtlenapped   9
3. The Wicked Witch of W. 73rd   19
4. Private Eye   29
5. Smudge   39
6. The A -Team   51
7. Spies   61
8. Weirdy Beardy   67
9. Turtle Soup   77
10. Thunk   85

BOOK 2: The Case with No Clues

1. Buried Treasure   97
2. Clue Number One   109
3. Hall of Presidents   115
4. The Ocean Blue   127

5.	Bobo Bars	135
6.	Newspaper	143
7.	Running Shoes	149
8.	The Zoo	159
9.	The Final Clue	171
10.	Pinecones	181
11.	I Pledge Allegiance	189
12.	Treasure Wherever You Go	201

BOOK 3: Bark at the Park

1.	Big Dog	213
2.	Cat's Out of the Bag	223
3.	Puppy Pals	229
4.	Cats Rule	239
5.	No Dogs Allowed	247
6.	Juicy Red	255
7.	Super-Duper Fired	263
8.	Mush	273
9.	Stadium Jail	281
10.	Dog of the Year	291

OTHER BOOKS
BY DUSTIN BRADY

Superhero for a Day: The Magic Magic Eight Ball

Trapped in a Video Game: Book One
Trapped in a Video Game: Book Two
Trapped in a Video Game: Book Three
Trapped in a Video Game: Book Four

ACKNOWLEDGMENTS

Special thanks to April Brady for the cover and interior illustrations. You can follow April's artwork on Instagram: @aprilynnart.

leila & nugget

MYSTERY 🐾 #1

who stole mr. t?

MISSING

MR T.

deserae & dustin brady

THE ABOMINABLE SNOW DOG

POOMF!

Kait laughed as her friend Leila's dog Nugget dove headfirst into the snow again. "That's soooo funny! He acts like he's never seen snow before!"

"It snowed a few times last year, but I don't think he remembers," Leila said. "He was just a puppy."

1

Nugget pulled his head out of the snow pile and looked at Leila and Kait. His face was one big snowball.

"He's the Abominable Snow Dog!" Kait giggled.

Leila had to laugh. Nugget did look funny. "Come on Mr. Abominable," she said. "We'll never finish our walk if you keep this up."

Nugget tilted his head at Leila, thought about what she'd said for a second, and — POOMF! — dove again.

"I think Nugget likes snow days even more than we do, and he doesn't even go to school!" Kait said.

Leila wasn't too sure about that. She hadn't been able to think about anything except for what she'd do on her snow day ever since she'd first heard about the possibility of a storm earlier that week. Leila never paid attention to the news when her parents watched, but the second the weather guy had said "snow," her head popped up from her book like Nugget's does whenever he hears the word "treat."

"Did he say something about a snowstorm?" Leila asked.

"Eight to twelve inches in some parts of the viewing area," TV weather guy said.

"Eight to twelve inches?!" Leila squealed.

"Don't count your chickens before they're hatched," Leila's mom warned.

Oh, the chickens would be counted. That week, the only thing that Leila and all the other students in Mrs. Pierce's third-grade class could talk about was their snow day plans. A lot of kids were going to the Memphis Road sledding hill. A few wanted to make money by shoveling driveways. The Heather Lane crew — Leila, Kait and their friend Javy — were going to have a snowball fight and build an igloo and make homemade snow cones and pull each other around on sleds and then maybe build a snowman or at least a snow dog. It was going to be quite a day.

The night before the big day, Leila's mom warned her about getting too excited. "They're always wrong about the weather, you know," she said.

"I know," Leila replied.

"It hasn't even started snowing yet."

"I know."

"Just plan on going to school tomorrow. That way it'll be a nice surprise if you get off."

"I know."

"Goodnight, Leila."

"Night mom."

Leila's mom shut off the light, and Leila lay awake for an hour thinking about how great the snow day would be. She finally drifted off to sleep, and the next thing she knew, something small and furry was rolling all over her bed.

"Nugget!" Leila's dad hissed. "Get down! Sorry honey, I just took him out, and…"

Leila didn't hear the rest because she'd just felt the dog with her hand. He was wet. And cold. She opened her eyes to see

Nugget's snow-covered face two inches from her nose. "Is it a snow day?!" Leila interrupted.

"It's 6:15 in the morning," Leila's dad said with a smile.

"IS IT A SNOW DAY?!"

"Yes, it's a snow day. Now why don't you go back to bed?"

Leila picked up Nugget and danced around her room. "Snow day! Snow day! Snow day!" Nugget licked her face, then ran to the heat vent to get warm. Leila couldn't fall back asleep because today was a snow day and snow days are the best days. She ran downstairs an hour before she'd normally wake up, devoured breakfast, then read a mystery book until her mom said it was OK to call Kait.

"Did you hear?!" she shouted into the phone.

"YES!" Kait yelled back.

"Call Javy!" Leila said. "I'll bring Nugget to your house, and then we'll walk to Javy's."

Leila and Kait had gotten about ten steps into their walk before Nugget started his snow-diving routine. At this pace, they'd never get to Javy's.

"It's OK," Kait said. "Javy might not even be awake yet. He didn't answer the phone."

"Why wouldn't he answer the phone?!" Leila asked. "Doesn't he know how much we have to do today?"

Kait stopped and stared at a piece of paper taped to a telephone pole. "Oh no," she said.

"What is it?" Leila asked as she leaned in to read the sign. "Ohhhh nooooooooooo."

"MISSING!" the sign said over a picture of a turtle.

NAME: MR. T
REWARD: ALL MY MONEY ($15.75)
CALL: 216-509-2212
ASK FOR JAVY MARTINEZ

2
TURTLENAPPED

Javy reached his house the same time Leila, Kait and Nugget did.

"Javy!" Kait yelled when she saw him. "What happened to Mr. T?!"

Javy slumped his shoulders and looked down. Nugget eyed the leftover fliers in his hand. "I don't know," Javy said. "I haven't seen him since I woke up this morning."

Nugget jumped and grabbed one of the fliers. He started wagging his tail, waiting for Javy to chase him. Javy just looked sad. Nugget stopped wagging his tail.

"Don't worry! We'll help you find him!" Kait said. "Right, Leila?"

"Oh, uh, yeah of course!" Leila said, a little worried about what this search might mean for the snowball fight.

"Really?" Javy asked. "That's great you guys! Come in." Javy opened the door and — *CRASH!* — knocked over a pile of boards inside the kitchen. "Yipes!" he said. "I'm so sorry!"

A construction worker with a big, wooly beard shook his head and helped Javy pile the boards back up. "My parents are getting the kitchen remodeled today," Javy explained to Leila and Kait as he finished stacking. "We'll have to be careful in here."

The kids picked their way through the maze of tools and wood until they got to a side room attached to the kitchen. "Here's Mr. T's winter home," Javy said.

Javy's family had turned their pantry into a turtle paradise. The walls were covered with pictures of Javy's family posing with Mr. T and drawings of the turtle dressed in funny costumes. A

wooden box piled high with dirt and moss took up every inch of floor space. The box held a small pool, a heat lamp, a few rocks and logs, but no turtle.

"What do you think happened?" Leila asked.

Javy looked at the two workers in the kitchen and lowered his voice. "Come to my room, and I'll tell you," he said.

The kids kept their boots on until they reached the dining room so they wouldn't get soggy socks from all the snow that had been tracked into the kitchen, then they turned into Javy's room. As soon as Nugget saw the carpet, he started pushing himself all over the floor to dry himself off. Kait started to take off her coat before thinking better of it. "It's cold in here," she said.

Javy nodded. "My dad likes to see how late in the year he can go without turning the heat on," he said. "He must be trying to beat his record."

"So when was the last time you saw Mr. T?" Leila asked, eager to find this turtle so they could get back on schedule with the snow day plans.

Javy plopped onto his bed. "Last night, he was in his home. I said goodnight and went to sleep. When I woke up this morning — poof! He was gone! I looked all over the house, but he's nowhere."

"What do you think happened?" Kait asked.

"I think he escaped," Javy said. "Sometimes we let him out so he can walk around the house. But when you do that, you've got to keep an eye on him. The construction guys have been going in and out of the house ever since they got here early this morning. I think they left the door open, and Mr. T ran away." Javy buried his head between his knees.

Kait moved closer and tried to make Javy feel better. "I mean, Mr. T is a turtle," she said with a smile. "He probably didn't *RUN* anywhere."

Javy sniffed a few times. "You know what I mean. I just don't know why he would want to leave in the first place. He hates the cold!"

Leila sat up. Javy had just reminded her of the book she'd been reading earlier that morning — *The Ice Cold Case*. It was a mystery that took place at a frozen pond (she'd picked it out in honor of the snow day). The detective in the book figured out that the thief was a raccoon by following prints in the snow. "If Mr. T went outside, we should be able to follow his tracks in the fresh snow, right?" Leila asked.

Javy perked up. "Oh yeah! That's a great idea!"

Leila left Nugget in the room so he wouldn't mess up the tracks, then led the way to the side door. She was feeling great about her plan until she looked down. The snow by the door was almost packed solid with footprints from the kids, the workers and Javy's parents. There was no way they could find turtle tracks in this mess. "Let's follow some of these away from the house where the snow isn't so packed," Leila suggested.

The biggest clump of tracks went down the driveway, so the kids followed those first. Unfortunately, they all ended at the bright red construction van parked at the end of the driveway. Next, they got excited when Kait spotted paw prints cutting across the front yard, but then Leila reminded everyone that's where they'd just walked with Nugget. Finally, they followed a set of prints that Javy guessed belonged to his dad going to the garage, but they didn't find any turtle tracks that way either.

"That's it," Javy said. "He must have gotten out before it started snowing. That was a good idea though, Leila."

"Bark! Bark!" Nugget had just spotted the kids through the bedroom window, and he seemed real upset that he hadn't been invited to the search party. He pressed his face up to the window, making a heart-shaped fog with his nose.

"OK, OK, we're coming," Leila said as she walked toward the window.

Kait, who'd been following close behind, grabbed Leila's arm. "Leila! Look!" She pointed to a single set of suspicious footprints that walked through Javy's backyard, to the back patio door, then left again into the neighbor's yard.

"Javy," Kait said. "What if Mr. T didn't run away at all?"

"What do you mean?" Javy asked.

Kait's eyes were wide. "What if he got turtlenapped?!"

3

THE WICKED WITCH OF WEST 73RD STREET

Kait gasped. "If Mr. T got turtlenapped, then this is a real-life mystery!" she exclaimed. Kait was trying to hide her excitement about the idea of a mystery in front of Javy, but the sparkle in her eyes gave her away.

Javy looked down. "I don't care about a mystery," he said. "I just want my friend back."

"Oh, we'll get him back," Kait said. "You know why? Because you're standing next to the best detective in town."

Javy looked up, surprised. "Leila?" he asked.

Leila gave Kait a weird look. "Detective? What are you talking about?"

Kait ignored her. "Leila's read basically every mystery book, so she knows all the tricks. Just the other day, she helped me solve the mystery of my missing Halloween candy."

"I reminded you that you ate it all," Leila said.

"See, isn't she good? She'll catch the turtlenapper before lunchtime!"

"Could you?" Javy asked hopefully.

Leila knew she was no detective, but she did very much want to find Mr. T in time to at least build an igloo. "We'll do our best," Leila said.

Kait squealed. "What do we do first?!"

Leila looked at the suspicious footprints. "We should probably follow these, right?"

"See?" Kait said to Javy. "Just like a real detective!"

The gang followed the footprints from Javy's back door, through the yard, past a row of bushes and into the neighbor's yard. Javy stopped when he saw which house the tracks had come from. "Mrs. Crenshaw." He shook his head. "I should have known."

"She doesn't like Mr. T?" Leila asked.

Javy pointed to the row of bushes they were standing next to. "These are Mrs. Crenshaw's rose bushes," he said. Then he pointed to a short wire fence next to the bushes. "And that's Mr. T's summer home. Every year, Mr. T figures out a way to eat half of Mrs. Crenshaw's roses through his pen, and every year she gets sooooo mad."

Leila scrunched up her face. "Mad

enough to break into your house and steal your pet?" she asked. "That's pretty mean."

"Oh, she's mean all right," Kait said. "SO mean! Remember that business I started a couple years ago? The one where I sold cool fall leaves?"

Leila remembered Kait's grandma giving her a quarter for some leaves Kait had found, which is not exactly a business, but she didn't argue. "I remember," Leila said.

"Well, Mrs. Crenshaw yelled at me for picking leaves off her tree! Can you believe it?"

"It is her tree," Leila pointed out.

"It was the FALL!" Kait exclaimed. "They were going to FALL off in a couple days anyways. She's like a witch, she's so mean!"

"That's not nice to say about

someone," Leila said. "It just sounds like she wants to keep her trees nice."

"Yeah, so she can use them for witch things," Kait mumbled.

"I wouldn't say she's a witch," Javy said, "But she's lived behind us ever since I was little, and I don't think she's come over even once. Don't you think it's suspicious that she shows up the very morning that Mr. T goes missing?"

Leila had to admit that it did seem odd.

"So how are we going to catch her?" Kait asked. Then her eyes lit up. "Do we get to spy?!"

Leila knew how much Kait loved spying on people, but she had a better idea. "How about we just ask her?" she said.

Kait made a face. "I'm not going over there," she said.

"Come on. I'll bring Nugget," Leila said.

Leila went back inside and got Nugget, who was more than happy to pounce in the snow again. Leila tugged on the leash to keep him moving. "Don't worry buddy," she said. "Soon we can play in the snow all we want." That gave her an idea. Maybe they could play in the snow and solve a mystery at the same time! She made a snowball and called Kait's name.

"What?" Kait asked as she turned around.

PIFF! It hit her square in the chest.

Kait giggled and threw a snowball at Javy. Javy did not join the fun. "Sorry guys. I wish I were in the mood to play, but I don't really feel like it right now. Why don't you two have a snowball fight, and I'll talk to Mrs. Crenshaw myself?"

Leila felt bad for taking Javy away from his search. "No Javy, we'll help you. Right Kait?"

Kait dropped the big, juicy snowball she'd been building. "Right. Of course."

Since Mrs. Crenshaw lived behind Javy and the kids felt she might get mad at them if they tromped through her backyard, they walked around the block to get to the front door.

"What do we say when we get there?" Javy asked.

"YOU'RE UNDER ARREST!" Kait yelled. "Then we handcuff her."

"We're not arresting anyone," Leila said. "Let's just ask her if she knows what happened to Mr. T."

"If she did take him, won't she just lie?" Javy asked as they rounded the corner onto W. 73rd St.

"If she tries to lie, she'll mess up and we'll catch her. That's what always happens in the books," Leila said, even though she had no idea how to catch someone in a lie.

"All I know is, if she answers the door riding on a broom, I'm running back home before she can get me," Kait said.

Leila rolled her eyes as she turned up Mrs. Crenshaw's driveway. "Be nice," she said. She scooped up Nugget right before they got to the door. She'd learned a long time ago that a small, waggly-tailed dog can make even the meanest adults nice.

Leila took a deep breath to gather her courage. The house was old and a little creepy. She stood in front of the door for a second and knocked. The door opened after just one knock, and a tall, skinny woman with straight, gray hair came to the door. She was holding a broom.

"What do you want?" she asked.

Kait stared at the broom for a moment before running off the porch.

4
PRIVATE EYE

Leila's face turned red. She did not expect her friend to be so embarrassing. "We're looking for his turtle," she finally said. "Can you help us?"

Mrs. Crenshaw looked at Leila and Javy, and then at Nugget, who even someone like Mrs. Crenshaw would have to admit looked pretty cute with his tongue sticking out. "Come in," she said.

"Oh no," Javy said. "It's OK, we were just..."

"Come in so I can close this door and stop letting all the heat out!" Mrs. Crenshaw snapped. Javy and Leila quickly stepped inside. "Take off your shoes," Mrs. Crenshaw instructed. They obeyed. "You two came at a good time. Can you hold this for me?" She handed Javy a dustpan.

"Oh, uh, sure," Javy said. While Javy helped Mrs. Crenshaw sweep the floor, Leila looked around. The house was brighter than she'd expected. Everything seemed to sparkle — especially the kitchen. She set Nugget down to explore. She knew she wouldn't be allowed to snoop around a stranger's house, but a cute, little doggy could get away with it. Maybe he'd find Mr. T or at least sniff out a clue. But as soon as Leila set him down, Nugget barreled for a tote bag in the kitchen. "Nugget!" Leila yelled after him. Too late. He'd already shoved his head and half his body inside, so when he looked at her, he was half-dog, half-bag.

"I'm sorry about my dog," Leila said as she ran over to Nugget. But before she could reach the bag, Nugget heard the heater turn on, shook off the bag and curled up in front of the vent.

Mrs. Crenshaw seemed to be losing patience with the two kids. "How can I help you?"

"We're looking for my pet turtle," Javy said. "Have you seen him?"

"Not since he finished off the last of my roses this summer," Mrs. Crenshaw answered flatly.

Javy's face turned red. "OK," he said as he turned to leave. "Thank you for your time."

Leila wasn't about to give up that easily. "This morning," she said. "Did you see him when you went to Javy's house this morning?"

That seemed to startle Mrs. Crenshaw, which made Leila happy. Good detectives are always startling people. "How did you know that?" Mrs. Crenshaw asked. "Were you spying on me?"

"Oh no!" Leila said. "I was just, uh, I mean…"

Javy jumped in. "Leila's a detective!"

he said.

That made Mrs. Crenshaw crack a small smile for the first time all morning. "A detective?"

Leila blushed. "Oh no, not really a detective. I mean, well you see, we just noticed footprints going from your house to Javy's back door. And so we were wondering what you were doing there this morning. That's all."

Mrs. Crenshaw tilted her head a bit, a full smile on her face now. "You followed footprints? That sure sounds like something a detective would do to me."

Leila blushed even redder if that were possible.

"Well," Mrs. Crenshaw said, "this morning, I recognized the red van in the Martinezes' driveway. It was the same company that helped me with my kitchen. Did you notice the name on the van?"

Leila shook her head.

"You need to pay attention to these things," Mrs. Crenshaw said. "That's what good detectives do. It's 'Margolis Construction.' Anyway, they did a good job on my kitchen, but they never took their shoes off and ended up tracking mud everywhere. It took me a week to scrub everything. I wanted to warn Mrs. Martinez so she wouldn't have the same problem."

"So you didn't take Mr. T?" Javy asked.

"No dear," Mrs. Crenshaw said. "That turtle and I are not friends, but I would never do anything like that."

"I know," Javy sighed. "I just really wanted to find him, and I thought maybe, I don't know…"

"It's OK," Mrs. Crenshaw said. "You've got to follow the clues. And I did actually see your turtle this morning."

"Really?!" Javy perked up.

Mrs. Crenshaw nodded. "While I was talking to your mom, I noticed your dad holding the turtle in the hallway."

"Oh wow!" Javy said. "Do you remember what time it was?"

"It was around 7:30."

"Thank you!" Leila said. "That's so helpful!"

"Aren't you going to write that down?" Mrs. Crenshaw asked.

"What do you mean?"

"It's a clue. You should write it down."

"Oh. Well, I don't really have pen or paper," Leila said.

Mrs. Crenshaw thought for a moment. "Let me get you something," she finally said. She walked upstairs, then came down a few minutes later with an old, hard-bound notepad that said "PRIVATE EYE" on the front. She flipped the crinkly pages until she found a blank one. "Why don't you use this?"

Leila wrote down a few clues from their conversation, then flipped through the book. It was filled with neat handwriting, a few drawings and lots of green check marks. "What is this?"

"When I was your age, I set up a detective agency in my neighborhood where I would solve cases for a nickel each. That was my detective notebook. I always knew how much money I'd made because each case I solved got a green check mark."

Leila flipped through the book again, counting all the check marks. "Wow! You were good!"

Mrs. Crenshaw allowed herself another smile. "To be honest, most of

my solutions came from books I was reading. Have you ever read Nancy Drew?"

"Of course!" Leila said. "All the ones at the library at least."

"I read all of them at least five times each," Mrs. Crenshaw said. Then she leaned in and raised an eyebrow. "I still have all of the originals if you ever want to borrow them."

"Wow!"

Mrs. Crenshaw turned back to Javy. "I'm sorry about your turtle," she said. "I know mysteries are no fun when you're the one who's lost a friend."

"We'll find him," Javy said.

Mrs. Crenshaw nodded. "Oh, I know you will. And when you do, we're going to teach him some rosebush manners!"

5
SMUDGE

Leila had her head buried in her notebook as she walked out of Mrs. Crenshaw's house. What could they be missing?

PIFF! A snowball hit her square in the face.

"Kait!"

"What?" Kait rejoined Leila and Javy from her hideout behind Mrs. Crenshaw's tree. "You wanted a snowball fight, right?"

"I'm trying to figure something out."

They walked in silence for a few seconds so Leila could think, then Kait whispered, "Did she try to cook you?"

"Excuse me?"

"The witch. Did she try to cook you?"

"OK, we can't be friends if you're going to keep calling people names," Leila said. "Her name is Mrs. Crenshaw. And in fact, she gave us an important clue. She saw Mr. T with Javy's dad at — let's see — 7:30 this morning."

"That's right before he leaves for work," Javy said.

"So your dad probably took the turtle to the vet or something on his way to work," Kait said.

Javy shook his head. "No way. I called him as soon as I woke up, and he didn't know where Mr. T was."

Kait looked at Javy out of the corner of her eye like she felt sorry for him, then said, "Well maybe… Never mind."

"What is it?" Javy asked.

"Well, what if he wasn't telling the truth?"

"Are you saying my dad would lie to me?"

"You're right, you're right. I'm sure he didn't. I barely even know your dad. He seems nice."

Leila shot a mean look at Kait. "Why would you say something like that?"

"Well, it's just... OK, one time my cousin Clara told me a story. You know my cousin Clara?"

Leila nodded. Cousin Clara was the one with all of the hard-to-believe stories.

"OK, well one time Clara told me about her friend Olivia who had a bunny named Smudge. She named him Smudge because he had a black smudge between his eyes that looked like someone had tried to erase something from his forehead. Anyways, Smudge was a great bunny, except he pooped everywhere. Like *EVERYWHERE*. And you know that bunny poops look kind of like chocolate candies and Olivia had a 2-year-old brother and…"

"I don't understand what this gross poo story has to do with Mr. T," Javy interrupted.

"I'm getting there," Kait said. "So one day, Smudge disappears. Olivia looks everywhere, but she never finds him. She figures he's run away and gives up looking. Then, a couple weeks later, she goes to Lake Farm Park — that's the field trip you go on in second grade where they let you milk the cow."

"We know," Leila said. Like Javy, she was also getting impatient with this story.

"Well sitting right next to the goats is a bunny rabbit that had a black smudge between his eyes. Turns out, it's Olivia's bunny. She finds out that her parents had gotten mad at the bunny and decided to give it away to the farm without telling her."

Javy looked horrified. Leila just shook her head. "So you're telling us the parents gave the bunny away because it pooped a lot? Couldn't they have just kept it in the cage more?"

Kait shrugged. "I mean it was pooping or chewing stuff or something. I forget exactly, but the point is the bunny was being bad, so her parents gave it away without telling her."

Javy was getting upset. "My dad would never give away Mr. T! He — he's been part of the family my whole life!"

Kait shrugged. "So was Smudge."

"You're not helping," Leila hissed at Kait. Then she turned to Javy and tried to calm him down. "That story probably wasn't true. Kait's cousin makes stuff up all the time. Let's focus on what we know. We know Mr. T was in the house at 7:30, right?"

Javy stopped panicking for a second to nod.

"And we know that there aren't any turtle tracks leaving the house, right?"

Javy nodded again.

"So he's probably still in the house!"

"Unless…"

That was all Kait could get out before Leila talked over her. "Why don't we all go back to the house and look for Mr. T again?"

Javy nodded. "That's a good idea. We can look for Mr. T until my dad comes home for lunch; then we can ask him what else he knows." While they walked back to the house, they decided that Javy would search the bedrooms, Kait would tackle the bathrooms and office, while Leila would take the living room and kitchen. "What about Nugget?" Javy asked. "Don't police use dogs to find missing people sometimes? Maybe Nugget can sniff out Mr. T?"

Leila looked at Nugget, who was jumping at falling snowflakes. "I don't think Nugget is that type of dog."

Javy wouldn't give up on his Nugget idea. When they got back to the house, he ran to Mr. T's home. "This is what the police do," Javy explained. "They have the dog sniff something from the missing person, so they know what they smell like." Then he paused. "Huh," he said.

"What is it?" Leila asked.

"I was going to have Nugget sniff Mr. T's cave — it's an upside down flowerpot that he likes to crawl into — but it's gone."

"Let's just start looking in our rooms," Leila suggested. Everyone agreed that would be best, and they split up. Leila started in the living room with Nugget. Nugget did a great job of searching the room, mostly because he was looking for snacks the whole time. He shoved his nose between cushions, squeezed behind the TV cabinet and Army crawled underneath the chair. No Mr. T, but they did find 57 cents in loose change, some goldfish snacks and a checker.

The kitchen was a little tougher because of all the construction, but Leila asked one of the workers for help. The guy with the beard seemed mean, so she asked one with a neck tattoo. He turned out to be nice. He moved boxes and opened cabinets for her, but they still couldn't find Mr. T. Fifteen minutes later, the kids met back in the living room. "Nothing," Leila said.

Javy was now wearing a too-big winter hat that covered half his head, making him look especially mopey. "I just found this hat. Are you guys cold too?"

Kait shook her head.

Leila wasn't about to give up. "How about the basement?"

"Mr. T doesn't walk down stairs," Javy said.

"But you never know!" Leila said. "We've got to check everywhere for clues!"

Javy shrugged, and they all walked downstairs. There wasn't much to Javy's basement. A washing machine and dryer stood against one wall, and tool shelves lined another. There were cleaning supplies in the corner, an old ping-pong table covered in boxes taking up the middle of the room, and that was about it. Leila walked around once, then started back up the stairs. Javy stopped her.

"Wait," he said. He walked to the ping-pong table and slowly pulled something out of a box. It was Mr. T's flower pot cave. He then took the box off the table and started sorting through it. It held all of Mr. T's possessions — food, toys, bowl, everything. It was exactly the type of thing someone would pack before giving away a turtle.

Just then a screen door closed upstairs. Javy's dad had come home for lunch.

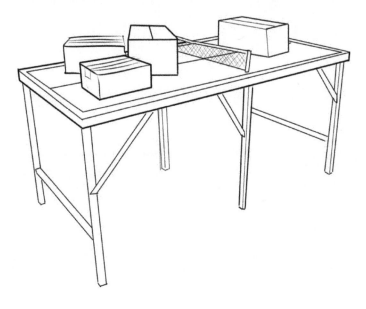

6

THE A-TEAM

Javy ran up the stairs with tears in his eyes. "DAD!" he yelled. "DAD, HOW COULD YOU?!"

"I told you," Kait said to Leila as she turned to follow Javy up the stairs.

"Save it," Leila mumbled.

Upstairs, Mr. Martinez had Javy wrapped in his arms. Nugget had also squeezed himself between the father and son, trying to get a free hug. "What's wrong?" Mr. Martinez kept asking.

"He was a good turtle!" Javy said between sobs. "He was such a good turtle! How could you give him away?"

"Give him away? I didn't give him away!" Mr. Martinez said. He looked at Javy, then at Leila and Kait. "Why would you even think that?"

"We followed the clues!" Kait said proudly.

"Clues? What clues?"

Javy laid out all the clues for his father the best he could between tears. "There aren't any turtle tracks outside (*sob*), and Mrs. Crenshaw saw you holding Mr. T this morning (*sob*), and then you packed all his stuff in a box to give away (*sob*)."

"Oh Javy," Mr. Martinez said. "I would never give Mr. T away. You know that."

"But the box…"

"I packed his stuff to keep it safe during the construction," Mr. Martinez said.

"But you're the only one who left the

house," Kait said. "And Mr. T isn't here, so you had to have taken him somewhere."

Mr. Martinez seemed annoyed for a second that the neighbor girl kept accusing him of lying, but he could see how upset this was making Javy. He took a breath and slowed things down a bit. "Javy, have I ever told you how Mr. T got in this family?"

Javy shrugged. "You got him a long time ago, right?"

"Not just a long time ago. I got him when I was exactly your age."

Leila gasped. "But that means that Mr. T must be…" she trailed off.

"Old?" Mr. Martinez offered.

Leila blushed.

"Mr. T is actually 32," Mr. Martinez said. "That's a pretty old pet, huh?"

Leila nodded.

"In third grade, I had a teacher named Mrs. Stanley. Mrs. Stanley was my favorite teacher ever, mostly because she kept a family of turtles right there in the classroom. She nicknamed the turtles the A-Team after the TV show."

Everyone stared blankly at Mr. Martinez.

"The A-Team? You guys know the A-Team, right? They'd make like flamethrowers out of gas pumps and... You know what? It's not important. The important thing is that Mrs. Stanley had a rule where if you got an 'A' on your homework, you got to help feed the A-Team that day. I wasn't always the best student, but I loved those turtles so much that I worked extra hard and crushed my homework that year. One turtle in particular was my favorite."

"Mr. T?" Javy asked.

Mr. Martinez nodded. "We started doing this thing where I would hold the food up in the air, and he would jump for it. He wouldn't do it for anyone else — just me."

"His jump trick?" Javy asked. "I thought all turtles did that."

"It's very rare," Mr. Martinez said. "Anyways, I started coming in early and staying late just to hang out with Mr. T. Mrs. Stanley must have noticed how much I'd bonded with the turtle because she took me aside one day after school and asked if I'd like to keep him. I was so excited that I dragged my mom to the store that night so we could buy every turtle toy they had. I don't think I slept for three nights. I just stayed up imagining all the adventures I'd have with Mr. T. Well, the day finally arrived when I was supposed to take Mr. T home. It was the last day of school before Christmas break. I showed up to school with a box that had Mr. T's name on it. Only he was gone."

Kait gasped.

"That's how I felt too," Mr. Martinez said. "Mrs. Stanley said that she'd been cleaning the cage that morning, and he just disappeared. She had the whole class search for Mr. T, but nobody found him. After a few hours, everybody else had forgotten about him. We had a party and watched a movie. It was the A-Team holiday special, which made me feel even worse. I remember that the heat was broken that day, so we all wore our coats in the classroom. I buried my head in my coat like a turtle and cried through the whole movie."

For the first time that day, Leila thought about how she'd feel if she ever lost Nugget. She decided that it must be the worst feeling in the world. "So what happened?" she asked.

"We never found him. The end-of-the-day bell rang, and I walked out of class behind a kid named Manny. Manny was part of the AV Club, which meant he helped the teacher wheel in the TV and hook up the video. I remember walking slowly as Manny pushed the TV cart and noticing that his video equipment bookbag looked weird. It had a big bulge in it. I looked closer. Then it started squirming. Manny's desk was next to mine because our last names were so close, and I remembered how jealous he'd been that I was getting Mr. T. I ran and got Mrs. Stanley, we opened the bookbag, and sure enough, there was Mr. T."

Kait gasped again. "Did you have him arrested?!"

"You know what? I couldn't get mad at him. He wouldn't even admit to taking the turtle, but I didn't care. That's how happy I was to have my buddy back." Then Mr. Martinez looked at his son. "Javy, I know how it feels to lose a best friend. Believe me, I'd never do that to you."

Javy hugged his dad. "I know, Dad."

During the hug, Leila brought out her detective notebook to write down a few more clues.

- A-Team
- Mrs. Stanley
- Manny

She paused and looked up. "Mr. Martinez, what was Manny's last name?"

"Margolis," he said.

Leila froze and stared at the first clue she'd written at the top of the page. She couldn't believe it. She may have just solved the case.

SPIES

"You OK?" Kait whispered to Leila. "You look like you're gonna hurl."

"I think I just solved the case," Leila whispered. "We need to talk to Javy. Alone."

"Hey Javy," Kait stuck her face between Javy and his dad. "You want to show us those snow fort plans now?"

"What snow fort plans?" Javy asked. "This is no time for a snow fort! We need to…"

Kait grabbed Javy's arm and started dragging him away. "They're in your room, right? Let's go!" Javy tried to push off, but Kait had a vice grip. "Don't wait for us, Mr. Martinez!" she said. "I know you've got to eat your lunch and get back to work! Yum yum!"

"Yum yum?" Leila asked when Javy's door closed behind them.

"Snow fort?!" Javy yelled. "I told you two — if you want to play in the snow, that's fine. But this is important to me! So you can…"

"Hush," Kait interrupted. "We just needed to get you in here. Leila solved the case."

Javy's eyes got wide.

"And just so you know, this is important to us too," Leila said. "I mean, I was really looking forward to the snow day, but you're my friend, and now I want to help you get Mr. T back more than anything."

"Thank you, Leila," Javy said. "Now

what did you find?"

Everyone's eyes were on Leila. Even Nugget had jumped onto the bed and was staring at her. She suddenly got a chill. "I, well, actually I'm pretty cold."

Kait threw Leila a blanket. "Just spit it out!" she said.

Leila wrapped up and settled down. "It's the first clue I wrote down," she said. "Look." She turned around her notebook to show Javy and Kait the name on the red van outside of Javy's house — **Margolis Construction.**

"Okayyyyy," Javy said.

"Manny's last name was Margolis," Leila explained.

Kait gasped. "The turtlenapper is back to finish the job!"

"But why would my dad hire Mr. Margolis if he knows he's a turtlenapper?" Javy asked.

"That's what I've been trying to figure out," Leila said. "Maybe it's a different Margolis."

Javy shook his head. "I don't think so. I heard my dad speaking Spanish with another man early this morning. I couldn't hear everything they were saying, but from the way they were talking, it sounded like they'd grown up together."

Kait held up her hand. "What about this — we know Mr. Margolis is a criminal, right? Maybe your dad hired him to help him pay for his crimes. Then your dad saw Mr. Margolis steal Mr. T this morning, but Mr. Margolis pulled out a gun and told him not to say anything!"

Javy, Leila and Nugget stared at Kait confused. Even for Kait, that was a pretty crazy idea. Finally, Leila spoke up. "Javy, I don't know why your dad trusts Mr. Margolis, but whatever the reason, I think it's up to us to catch him."

"But how?" Javy asked. "Do we question him?"

"NO!" Kait shouted. "WE SPY!"

Leila sighed. "I hate to say it, but Kait might be right this time. I think we need to spy."

Kait pumped her fist. "Yes! OK Javy, we need binoculars and a listening device. If you don't have a real spy listening device, a glass cup should do. Now, do you…"

Leila stopped Kait right there. "No

binoculars," she said. "We need to get close enough to search their stuff."

Kait folded her arms across her chest. "Well, I only do far-away spying."

"Bark! Bark!" Everyone turned to Nugget. He was standing on the edge of the bed, wagging his tail. "Bark!"

Javy laughed. "Nugget looks like he's ready to help."

Leila nodded. "And I think I know just the way."

8

WEIRDY BEARDY

The kids waited until Javy's dad was ready to go back to work.

"Javy, I'm leaving!" Mr. Martinez shouted from the kitchen. "Do I get a hug goodbye?"

Kait slapped Javy on the shoulder, and he marched to the kitchen. Leila, Kait and Nugget waited in the bedroom while Javy said goodbye to his dad and then secretly scattered chunks of string cheese throughout the kitchen. A minute later, he came back to the room and nodded. Leila then whispered Nugget's three favorite words into the dog's ear. "Find the treats!"

Nugget tore out of the room and sprinted through the house until he found the first chunk of cheese in the dining room. He leaped over a pile of tile on the ground and continued his search inside the kitchen. "I'm so sorry!" Kait said to the startled workers who had to pause what they were doing when a small, furry bullet bounded over them and started sniffing everything in sight.

The three kids ran through the room, pretending to chase Nugget while they really searched every nook and cranny for signs of turtlenapping.

"Nugget, come back!" Javy yelled while he poked his head into a toolbox.

"You're not being a good dog!" Leila said as she opened a cabinet. She made sure to yell the "good dog" part of the sentence extra loud so Nugget knew he was doing a great job.

Kait flipped a cardboard box upside down, dumping out covers for power outlets and heater vents. "I can use this box to catch him!" she announced. When she found nothing interesting inside, she moved onto another box. *Dump*. "Or maybe this would be better!"

The two workers (whom Kait had earlier nicknamed "Weirdy Beardy" and "Tattoo Tom") waited patiently while the little show in front of them finished up. When the kids finally decided that the turtle was no longer in the kitchen, Leila swooped Nugget into her arms and apologized to the workers. Time for Part Two of the plan.

For Part Two, the kids bundled up and went outside to build a snow fort. But this wasn't the fort they'd been planning for the last week. No, this would be their special base to sneak into the real target — the van. Once they finished the fort, Leila curled up with Nugget inside while Javy and Kait crouched nearby. For a few minutes, everything was silent. Leila's heart was pounding. This was the most exciting snow day she could have ever imagined!

At that moment, Weirdy Beardy walked out of the house toward the van. Leila took a sharp breath. This was it! Any second now, Kait should be starting a snowball fight with Javy. She'd hit him and run toward the van. Then Javy would throw a snowball back at her, but he'd throw it way over her head on purpose. When Javy would let go of the snowball, Leila would release Nugget, who'd chase the snowball into the van. Finally, the kids would follow Nugget into the van and find Mr. T. It was, they'd all agreed, the perfect plan.

PIFF!

"Ow!" Javy shouted. "Hey, you didn't need to throw it in my face," he muttered.

"Focus, guys," Leila hissed from her snow fort.

"Haha, can't catch me!" Kait ran

toward the van just as Weirdy Beardy opened its back door. Javy made a snowball, wound up and threw it at the van. "Go!" Leila said as she turned Nugget loose. Nugget got low to the ground and barreled after the snowball. Javy had thrown a perfect lob. The snowball was just about to land inside the van, when —

SLAM!

Weirdy Beardy closed up the van, and…

PIFF!

The snowball hit the back door. Nugget stared at the snow spot on the van and then looked back at Leila. Weirdy Beardy walked out the side of the van with a long, plastic tube under his arm.

Leila jumped out of her snow fort. "Oh no!" she shouted. Weirdy Beardy didn't even notice her as he walked into the house.

"What do we do now?" Javy asked.

"I, I don't know," Leila said as she picked up Nugget. "We could try it again when they come back out, but they'll be expecting it this time. Should we call the police? They probably won't come. Oh boy. Uh, well we could..."

While Leila's mind was spinning in circles, Kait calmly walked to the van's back door and opened it. "Coming?" she asked.

Leila and Javy stared with their mouths open.

"He didn't lock it. You should have noticed that, detective. Come on."

"I don't know," Leila finally said. "If Nugget goes in first, I feel like it's OK to chase him inside, but isn't this breaking into somewhere we don't belong?"

"How can it be breaking in? They're at Javy's house. You're allowed to look inside anything at your own house. It's the law." With that, she walked in. Javy looked at Kait, then back at Leila, then jumped into the van.

Leila didn't know much about the law, but she was almost positive that's not the way it works. She was just about to turn around when Nugget squirmed out of her arms and jumped into the van. "Nugget, wait!" She followed the dog inside but stopped short when she found Kait and Javy tearing through boxes and equipment. "Guys, come on," she said. "We shouldn't be doing this. Mr. T probably isn't even…" she stopped midsentence when her eyes landed on a small cooler with a turtle logo on it.

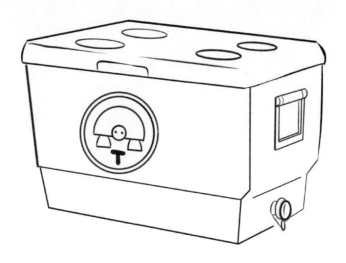

Javy gasped. "Mr. T!" he shouted. Before he could tear open the cooler, however, a figure appeared in the doorway.

"What are you kids doing in my van?!"

TURTLE SOUP

"AHHHHH!" Kait screamed.

"Hey, it's OK," the man said.

"AHHHHH!"

The man's expression changed from anger to concern. "Really, it's OK. I'm not going to hurt you."

"AH! AH! AHHHHHH!" Kait's face was turning red.

The man looked around nervously. "Come on, people are going to think I'm kidnapping you or something. Get out of the van, and we can talk in the house."

Kait instantly stopped screaming. "OK," she said as she climbed out.

Leila scooped up Nugget and nodded at Javy, who pulled his home's cordless phone from his coat pocket and made a quick call. When Leila hopped out of the van, she noticed a Margolis Construction pickup truck parked in the driveway that hadn't been there before. That must be where the man had come from.

Back in the house, the man sat across from the kids at the dining room table. "So now can you tell me why you were snooping in my van?"

Kait stuck her nose up in the air. "Only if you first tell us why you're stealing turtles."

"Wait, what are you talking about?"

Leila decided to jump in. "Are you Manny Margolis?"

"I am."

"You stole my dad's turtle in third grade," Javy shouted. "And you almost got away with stealing him again!"

"OK," Mr. Margolis held up his hand. "I've told your dad a million times — I did NOT steal that turtle in third grade."

Kait rolled her eyes. "Oh please. We're kids, but we're not stupid. It's pretty hard to not notice a giant turtle in your bookbag."

"Listen," Mr. Margolis said. "First of all, that wasn't my bookbag. That was the AV room bookbag, so I didn't know what was inside. Second, Mrs. Stanley was in the room with me the whole time I was setting up, so she would have noticed me stealing a turtle. Third..." Mr. Margolis shook his head. "I don't know why I'm explaining all this to you. You're not going to believe me now, just like no one believed me back then. Go ahead. Open the cooler and see for yourself."

Javy opened the cooler, looked inside, then slumped his shoulders. "It's soup," he said.

"Soup?!" Kait screeched. "You turned

Mr. T into soup?! YOU MONSTER!"

Weirdy Beardy popped his head into the dining room. "Is that my soup?" His eyes lit up when he saw the cooler in front of Javy. "Thanks! I was looking all over for this! I'm starving!" He grabbed the cooler and walked out of the dining room.

"I'm super sorry," Leila said.

"It's OK," Mr. Margolis said. "I just wish you would have talked to me rather than look through my stuff. There's some expensive equipment in there. Plus, breaking into someone else's vehicle is a crime, you know."

Leila shot Kait a glare. Then she looked around the room. "Has anyone seen Nugget?"

"Great!" Kait said. "Now we've got two missing animals? Does this house just eat pets?!"

"Here he is." Javy's dad walked into the room holding Nugget. "He was curled up in front of the living room heater." He gave Nugget to Leila and turned to Javy. "Now what's the big emergency that you had to call me home from work?"

"We thought Mr. Margolis had taken Mr. T, but we were wrong," Javy said.

"Why would you think he took Mr. T? Manny's one of my oldest friends!"

"Because he stole Mr. T when you were in third grade! We thought the only reason he'd be here is if he were finishing the job!"

Javy's dad shook his head. "You don't stay mad at someone forever just because they do something one time. You forgive people. Mr. Margolis was one of my best friends all through school. That's why I hired him to do our kitchen!"

"Well that was our last idea," Javy said. "We'll never find Mr. T now."

Something about this whole thing had been bothering Leila ever since Javy's dad had handed her Nugget. Finally, she realized what it was — Nugget was toasty warm. "Mr. Martinez," she said. "Has the heat been on all day?"

Javy's dad looked puzzled. "Of course. It's been on since last week. Why do you ask?"

Leila smiled. "I think I just solved two cases."

THUNK

Leila sprinted down the steps to Javy's basement while everyone else tried to keep up. "Leila, I told you — Mr. T can't walk down stairs!" Javy said.

"I know that," Leila replied. "He's not in the basement."

"What are you talking about?!" Kait asked.

Without answering, Leila grabbed a broom and looked at the ceiling. Javy's basement didn't have any ceiling tiles, which meant Leila had a clear view to all the pipes above. She walked across the room to where she guessed the kitchen

was and started banging pipes with the handle of her broom.

CLANG!

She walked forward a step and banged again.

CLANG!

She took another step and tried one more time.

THUNK.

Leila tried twice more.

THUNK. THUNK.

"Why does it sound like that?" Javy asked.

Leila smiled. "Because there's a turtle in there!"

Javy's eyes got wide. "No way!"

"Let's go up to your bedroom and find out if I'm right!"

Nugget led the way by galloping up the stairs. Mr. Margolis grabbed a screwdriver from the kitchen and quickly unscrewed the heater vent from the bedroom wall. Javy reached inside. "Feel anything?" his dad asked.

"No," Javy said. Then he reached in a little farther. "Wait!" He leaned in as far as he could, smooshing his face against the wall. He gasped. "Mr. T!" He finally scooped out the turtle. Mr. T was a little dusty from the vent, but alive and looking quite pleased with himself.

"Mr. T, I can't believe you're OK!" Javy gave Mr. T a giant hug, or at least as big of a hug as he could give the turtle with Nugget squeezed in between.

"I'm so confused!" Kait said. "Did Mr. Margolis hide the turtle in there so he could take him later?"

"NO!" Leila and Mr. Margolis shouted at the same time.

"It was all Nugget," Leila explained while she petted her dog. "He loves curling up by the heater when he comes in from the cold. He's done it all day — at my house, in Mrs. Crenshaw's house and in the living room just now. I just remembered that the only place he hasn't done it is Javy's bedroom. That's because no heat has been coming out of the vent. Notice how cold it is in here compared to the rest of the house? Mr. T's been blocking the heat to this room all day!"

"But how did he get in there in the first place?" Javy asked.

"From the kitchen!" Leila was practically bouncing in place, she was so excited. "Your dad had to let Mr. T out of his turtle home this morning to put his stuff away when the construction guys came. Well, it got cold with them opening the door a bazillion times. We know Mr. T hates the cold — that's why he has a heat lamp and a flower pot cave in his home. So he went to the warmest cave he could find. Kait, do you remember what fell out of the first box you dumped in the kitchen this afternoon?"

Kait's eyes got wide. "The covers for the kitchen heater vents!"

Leila nodded. "So Mr. T crawled into

the duct and tried walking toward Javy's voice."

"I can't believe he was right here the whole time!" Javy said.

"You said you solved two mysteries," Mr. Margolis said. "Does that mean you figured out what happened to Mr. T when I was in third grade?"

Leila nodded. "Just like today, it was cold then too. Remember? The heat was broken. While the teacher was cleaning Mr. T's cage, he must have hidden in the warmest cave he could find."

"The bookbag!" Mr. Margolis exclaimed.

Javy's dad turned in shock. "So you really didn't steal Mr. T back then?!"

"That's what I've been telling you for the last 30 years!" Mr. Margolis said.

The two men did a complicated handshake and hugged. "I should have never doubted you," Javy's dad said.

"And I never should have toilet papered your house to get back at you for doubting me," Mr. Margolis said.

"That was you?!"

"That's THREE mysteries solved!" Kait exclaimed.

"Hey, does anyone know what time it is?" Javy asked.

Kait looked at her watch. "It's 3:30."

"Good."

"Why 'good'?" Kait asked.

"Because that leaves me two hours of daylight to get back at you for hitting me in the face with a snowball."

"You've got to catch me first!" Kait squealed as she ran out of the bedroom.

Nugget sprinted after her, excited to finally enjoy the snow day he'd been promised.

One week later, Leila was wiping

cookie crumbs off her face in Mrs. Crenshaw's kitchen as she wrapped up her story. "Mr. Margolis finished the kitchen remodel a few days later, and he even added some extra stuff to Mr. T's room to make it cooler," she said.

"That's wonderful," Mrs. Crenshaw said. "But you never finished your story. Did he ever catch her?"

"Did who catch who?"

"Did Javy ever catch up to Kait and get her back?"

"Oh yeah," Leila said. "We had the biggest snowball fight ever that afternoon! Toward the end, Javy used Nugget to lure Kait into a trap behind the shed, then he hit her with a snowball so big it could have been a snowman's head!"

Mrs. Crenshaw sat back and chuckled. "Good for him."

"Well anyways, here's your notebook back," Leila said as she slid the old "Private Eye" notebook across the table. "It was great."

"No no, I want you to keep it," Mrs. Crenshaw said. "You're the new detective on the block, now."

"Really?!" Leila asked. "I mean, I don't know if I'm really a detective."

"You don't know if you're a detective?" Mrs. Crenshaw asked. "Did you solve a case?"

"Well, yeah, but…"

"Then you're a detective. End of story. You don't need someone to give you a title for it to be true. Now, did you read any of the other cases in the notebook?"

"Oh! What? Uhhhh, I mean…" Leila wasn't normally a snooper like Kait, but if someone hands you a notebook full of real-life mysteries, what are you supposed to do?

"It's OK," Mrs. Crenshaw said. "You probably noticed that all of the cases had green check marks next to them except for one."

Leila had noticed. She flipped back to it. "The Case With No Clues." While most of the other cases in the book had just a handful of notes written underneath the title, this one had four whole pages of questions, maps, arrows and lots of scribbles.

Mrs. Crenshaw tapped the notebook. "Think you want to give this one a try?"

Leila stared at the title for a second, then looked up, confused. "There aren't any clues?"

"No clues," Mrs. Crenshaw said with a twinkle in her eye. "But there is a treasure."

leila & nugget
MYSTERY #2

the case with no clues

deserae & dustin brady

1
BURIED TREASURE

"Thanks, Miss Carol!" Leila said to the bus driver as she jumped the last step out of the bus and ran toward her house.

"Wait up!" Leila's friend Kait yelled.

Leila sighed and slowed down.

"Want to do something fun?" Kait asked when she caught up.

"Sorry, can't," Leila answered, still on the move.

Kait continued as if she hadn't heard Leila. "I think I can make my brother play with us today. If not, I have an idea for a new way to spy on my sister. Or, hey, did I tell you about that five-pound gummy bear I saw online? Maybe we could…"

"I'm really sorry," Leila replied, speeding up again.

"Come on!" Kait struggled to keep up. "Whatever it is can't be that important."

Oh, it was definitely that important. Leila had been counting down the minutes to this moment ever since math class had ended at 10:30. That was five hours ago, and five hours is a really long time to count down to anything. Her elderly neighbor, Mrs. Crenshaw, had promised to tell her about a super-old mystery and hidden treasure this afternoon. A hidden treasure! Just like the movies! Leila got butterflies in her tummy every time she thought about it. "See you tomorrow!" Leila yelled over her shoulder as she ran up her driveway.

Inside the house, she hugged her mom, hugged her little dog Nugget and said the five magic words: "Wanna go for a walk?" Nugget leaped high enough to touch Leila's nose with his own. Leila smiled, clipped on the leash and ran the whole way to Mrs. Crenshaw's house.

Mrs. Crenshaw had opened the door before Leila got to the porch. "Come in, Miss Detective! I've been waiting for you."

Nugget looked up and wagged his tail, hoping for a treat. Mrs. Crenshaw pulled a dog biscuit out of her pocket. "Yes, I've been waiting for you too," she said. Nugget wagged his tail harder and stood on his back legs as Mrs. Crenshaw flipped him the treat.

Before Nugget could even swallow the biscuit, Leila had sat at the kitchen table and opened her detective notebook to the unsolved case. "I'm ready!"

"I have cookies in the oven," Mrs. Crenshaw said. "Don't you want to wait until they're ready?"

"Noooooooooo!" Leila pretended to melt in her seat. "You've got to tell me now! I've been dying ever since we talked yesterday!"

Mrs. Crenshaw laughed. "OK, OK," she said. "I suppose I owe you." Mrs. Crenshaw grabbed an old school yearbook from the counter and flipped through it until she landed on a black-and-white picture of a man with thick glasses, a thin mustache and a gleam in his eye. "Do you know who this is?"

Leila shook her head.

"This is Mr. McGee. He was the first principal at Englewood Elementary School."

"That's where I go to school!" Leila exclaimed.

Mrs. Crenshaw smiled and nodded. "I went there too," she said. "Look." She flipped a few pages and pointed to a girl with tight curls and a smile that was

almost too big for her face. "That little girl was never more excited for anything in her life than she was for June 4, 1947 — the last day of third grade. That was the day of the treasure hunt."

Leila scooted forward in her chair. Finally, the good stuff.

Mrs. Crenshaw continued. "Mr. McGee was the best principal. There were more than 400 kids in school, and Mr. McGee had nicknames for every single one of them. I was Nance, after Nancy Drew, because I was so good at solving mysteries. Mr. McGee loved mysteries, and he loved surprises. He loved them so much that a few weeks before my third-grade year ended, he announced that he'd have a special mystery for the whole school to solve together on the last day of school. It would be a treasure hunt, and the student who found the treasure first got to keep it."

"What was the treasure?"

"Mr. McGee wouldn't tell anyone," Mrs. Crenshaw said. "It was probably just some little trinket, but people started saying that they'd heard Mr. McGee had buried a treasure chest under the playground or he'd inherited a bunch of gold coins or he secretly owned a toy store. One boy was even going around school telling everybody that Principal McGee used to be a pirate."

Leila wrote, "Pirate?" in her notes and looked back up.

Mrs. Crenshaw continued. "On the last day, everyone was buzzing. A lot of kids brought magnifying glasses or dressed up as Sherlock Holmes. The pirate boy wore a patch. We all gathered at the flagpole for our first clue. We waited and waited, but Mr. McGee never showed up. One of the teachers finally got word that his wife had gotten sick, and Mr. McGee had gone to the hospital with her in the middle of the night. The treasure hunt was canceled."

"That stinks," Leila said. "But you were able to do the treasure hunt the next year, right?"

Mrs. Crenshaw shook her head. "Mrs. McGee's health got worse. They moved across the country that summer so she could get better care."

Leila was starting to understand. "So the treasure stayed hidden."

"Everyone else forgot about it, but I couldn't," Mrs. Crenshaw said. "I looked all over the school for clues. I thought that if I could just find one, I'd be able to pick up the trail and solve the mystery. I stayed an hour after school for a month straight, searching classrooms, questioning teachers and reading about famous treasure hunts. I even started digging in the corner of the playground before the janitor noticed and made me stop."

"But you never found it?"

"Nobody's found it."

"And you think I can find it? After 70 years? With no clues or anything?!" This wasn't exactly the news Leila had been hoping for.

"I know it probably won't happen," Mrs. Crenshaw said. "After 70 years, the clues are almost definitely gone by now. I just remember how much fun I had treasure hunting, and I thought you'd enjoy it too. Plus, it's going to be gone for good in a few months."

Leila nodded. After 78 years, Englewood Elementary was finally getting a new building. When Leila's bus passed the construction site for the new school every morning, she always strained to catch a glimpse of the progress on its gigantic playground. By June, the current school building would be nothing but a memory.

Leila sighed. "OK," she said. "I'll take the case. It doesn't hurt to look, right?"

Even though Leila was reluctant to start, the mystery soon sucked her in. Mrs. Crenshaw was right — treasure hunting was a lot of fun. Before Leila knew it, she was memorizing every half-clue and maybe-clue Mrs. Crenshaw had written down as a kid. She secretly scoured every dusty corner and tall cabinet in the school for anything that looked old. She talked to Nugget so much about the case that even he seemed to get tired of it.

After a few weeks of no clues, though, Leila's interest in the treasure started to fizzle. Sure, she wanted to find it, but she had to face the facts — the trail was gone. Other cases started to crowd the treasure out of her mind. Every day, the new building was looking more like a school, and every day, Leila cared less that the old building and its treasure were going to be gone soon. After two months, Leila had all but forgotten about treasure hunt mystery.

That all changed the day she found clue number one.

2

CLUE NUMBER ONE

Leila wasn't even trying to find the hidden treasure the day she stumbled upon the first clue. She was working on a completely different mystery that morning — the Case of How to Stay Awake During the World's Most Boring History Lesson.

"And this is Millard Fillmore," Leila's teacher, Mrs. Pierce, said as she changed the picture on the screen. "He was the thirteenth president. He installed the first bathtub in the White House. Here's a picture of that bathtub."

Mrs. Pierce could make any lesson exciting — especially history — but even she was struggling with the "Presidents You've Never Heard Of" chapter. "And this is Grover Cleveland. He actually served two different terms in the White House. Can you imagine being president two different times?"

Yup. Leila could imagine it pretty easily. Her eyelids started drooping, so she concentrated on the picture of Grover Cleveland to stay awake. She stared at his bushy mustache and bowtie. She wondered what it would be like to have the name, "Grover." Wait, was this the guy who invented Cleveland? Her eyelids were getting heavy again.

Then, Mrs. Pierce changed the picture again, and Leila gasped out loud.

"This is William Henry Harrison," Mrs. Pierce said. "He was president for the

shortest amount of time — only 31 days."

Leila's hand shot up.

"Yes, Leila!" Mrs. Pierce said, beaming. She seemed happy that at least one person in the class was paying close enough attention that they would have a question.

"Did William Henry Harrison have

anything to do with our school?" Leila asked.

Mrs. Pierce looked confused. "Well, he died long before our school was built, and I don't think he ever visited our town. Why do you ask?"

"No reason!" Leila said, her face turning red. "Silly question!"

But it wasn't a silly question. Leila had seen the face somewhere before, and she was almost positive she'd seen it at the school. But where? It took her another two minutes to figure it out, and when she did, she gasped again. The girl in front of her turned around to give her a dirty look. "Sorry," Leila mouthed.

With the building closing for good at the end of the school year, the principal had decided to dig up a bunch of old stuff from Englewood Elementary's history and display it in the hallways.

Leila had spent hours studying the pictures and knick-knacks because she knew they were probably her only chance of finding the clues that Mr. McGee had hidden all those years ago.

One of the things she'd studied for a whole week was the staff picture collection. Every year, the school displayed a group picture of all of the school's teachers in the hallway next to the office. Leila was never sure why the school did that — maybe so students wouldn't forget what their teacher looked like? This year the school had lined an entire hallway with staff pictures going back to the 1940s. Leila spent the longest time staring at the 1947 picture to learn whatever she could about the year of the treasure hunt. Turns out, Mr. McGee had hidden a very important clue in the picture.

The moment school let out, Leila ran for the picture. She had to see if she was right. When she got there, she caught her breath. In the second row of the picture, surrounded by 120 serious teachers, was the face of a man who'd died 100 years before the picture was even taken. It was President William Henry Harrison.

3

HALL OF PRESIDENTS

When Kait sat next to Leila on the bus, she gave her friend a weird look.

"You OK?" Kait asked.

"Uh, yeah! Of course!" Leila said.

"Cuz you're doing that face that people make on Scooby-Doo when they've seen a ghost."

"Oh! Haha! Weird!" Leila said. She wanted so much to tell someone about her discovery, but she knew that if she told Kait, the whole school would know in about two seconds, and she needed to keep this secret a little longer — at least until she could ask Mrs. Crenshaw about it.

Kait frowned at Leila like she didn't believe her, but she decided to drop it. The two girls went their separate ways off the bus. Leila walked to her house like everything was normal, but as soon as she stepped inside, she started running.

Her mom tilted her head after Leila gave her the world's fastest hug. "What's got you so excited?" she asked.

"I just found a big clue in a case!" Leila said, fumbling with Nugget's leash. "A BIG clue! I've got to tell Mrs. Crenshaw!"

"OK," Leila's mom said. "Just make sure you're home in time for dinner."

"Of course!" Leila shouted, already two steps out the door. Nugget matched her step-for-step as she raced to Mrs. Crenshaw's house. When she reached the front door, she started knocking and knocking.

Mrs. Crenshaw came to the door, annoyed. "What?" she asked harshly before looking down to see Leila and Nugget.

"The first clue!" Leila gasped. "I found the first clue!"

Mrs. Crenshaw's face softened, and she opened the door. "The first clue to what, dear? That missing stuffed animal you've been helping your friend find?"

"THE TREASURE!" Leila squealed, skipping into the house.

Mrs. Crenshaw's eyes got wide. Nugget bounded around the room in glee — not that he knew what was going on, but everyone was so excited that he had to bound. After a full minute, both Leila and Nugget calmed down enough that Leila could finally tell Mrs. Crenshaw the whole story of her discovery. "Can you believe it?!" Leila asked when she'd finally finished.

Mrs. Crenshaw folded her arms across her chest. She looked like she wanted to believe it, but she wasn't convinced yet. "Are you sure it was President Harrison?" Mrs. Crenshaw asked. "It's a blurry, old picture, and a lot of blurry, old pictures look the same."

"Very sure!" Leila exclaimed. "Surer than sure! If you look really close at the picture, you can see where Principal McGee cut around the president's head and glued it on there. But what could it mean?!"

"The Hall of Presidents," Mrs. Crenshaw said.

"What's that?"

"Principal McGee was very big on history, so he lined the whole east hallway of the school with pictures and facts about U.S. presidents — from

Washington all the way to Truman. This clue must be saying that the next clue is hidden behind Harrison's picture."

Leila's shoulders slumped. "But that picture isn't there anymore."

"Right."

"Oh."

"I'm sorry, honey. But that was an excellent job finding the first clue! In 70 years, you're the only person who's ever noticed it."

Leila was too deep in thought to take the compliment. "But what if the clue's still there?"

Mrs. Crenshaw shook her head. "That picture of Harrison is long gone. Nobody's keeping a poster that old."

"But what if the clue wasn't on the poster? What if it was somewhere nearby?"

Mrs. Crenshaw shrugged. "Even so,

it's not going to last 70 years."

"This clue did!" Leila was warming up to this idea. "Do you remember where Harrison would have been in the hallway?"

"I could figure it out, but…"

"Please? Oh please, could you show me?!"

Even though Mrs. Crenshaw was shaking her head, a tiny sliver of her mouth had turned up into a smile, giving her away.

Leila saw that sliver and knew that Mrs. Crenshaw wanted to find this treasure just as much as she did. "Pleeeeeeeeease?"

Mrs. Crenshaw huffed. "My nephew's the school janitor. I suppose I could give him a call."

"Yay!" Leila danced around the room. "Nugget, we're going for a ride!" Nugget danced too.

Mrs. Crenshaw called her nephew, Leila called her mom, and five minutes later, they were ready to leave. Mrs. Crenshaw eyed Nugget as she unlocked her car. "He's not going to shed all over my seats, is he?"

"Oh no!" Leila exclaimed. "He's a cavapoo!"

"A what?" Mrs. Crenshaw asked with squinty eyes.

"Cavapoo! That means he's part poodle, so he doesn't shed!"

Nugget looked up and wagged his tail proudly.

Mrs. Crenshaw thought about it for another few seconds, then sighed. "I've never let a dog in my car before. He'd better watch himself."

"He will! I'll make sure of it!" Leila scooped Nugget into her arms and sat on the spotless back seat of Mrs. Crenshaw's car.

Three minutes later, they arrived at the school. "OK, Nugget, you be good in here," Leila said as she left the dog in the car. "We'll just be gone for a few minutes."

Nugget scrambled to the door and watched Mrs. Crenshaw and Leila walk away. He pressed his nose to the window, fogging it all up. Mrs. Crenshaw turned and shook her head at Nugget. He stared back at her, wagging his tail and fogging the window more.

"Is he going to keep doing that?" Mrs. Crenshaw asked.

"Oh yeah," Leila said. "He's going to stay right there until we come back."

Mrs. Crenshaw rolled her eyes and walked back to the car. "We'd better bring him with us then," she said.

Leila's eyes got big. "You mean it's OK to take a dog into the school?"

"It's going to have to be OK," Mrs. Crenshaw said. "I don't want him snotting all over my windows."

Leila opened the door, and Nugget leaped out, overjoyed that he got to join the adventure.

"Keep him on a leash and let me do any talking," Mrs. Crenshaw said.

The janitor, Mr. Peterman, was taking down the flag for the day when Leila, Nugget and Mrs. Crenshaw walked up. He looked down at Nugget. "Oh no, Aunt Margaret! You didn't tell me…"

"It'll be fine, Daniel," she said. "The dog's housetrained, and he's a something-poo that doesn't shed."

"Cavapoo," Leila added helpfully.

Mrs. Crenshaw didn't wait for permission from the stunned Mr.

Peterman - she just took the key out of his hand and unlocked the school door. Leila hurried to join her as she started walking down a long hallway. "Harrison was the ninth president, so his picture would be nine doors down on the left," Mrs. Crenshaw said. Leila counted off the doors until they got to the music room. The three of them stared at a bulletin board decorated with smiling musical notes.

"Well, this is it," Mrs. Crenshaw finally said.

"OK, so maybe the clue is underneath the decorations on the board," Leila suggested.

"It's not," Mrs. Crenshaw said. "This bulletin board wasn't even here when I was in school."

"So maybe it's on the wall behind the bulletin board!"

"For one thing, no. It's not. For another, I didn't bring my power tools to remove a bulletin board. Did you?"

Leila wasn't about to give up after coming all this way. "Well, maybe it's in the room behind the wall!"

Mrs. Crenshaw sighed. "We can check."

Leila, Nugget and Mrs. Crenshaw spent the next half hour searching the music room. Nugget found lots of crumbs to gobble up, but that was about it. Finally, Leila sighed. "I guess it's not in here," she said. "I'm sorry Mrs. Crenshaw. You were right. I guess I just really wanted to find that clue."

"It's OK, dear," Mrs. Crenshaw said. "I did too." They walked out to the hallway and stared at the bulletin board one last time. Nugget, who was still in crumb-finding mode, put his nose to the ground and started sniffing. He sniffed closer and closer to the wall. Then, he suddenly started sniffing like crazy and pawing at one of the bricks.

"Nugget!" Leila said. "Don't be bad! There's nothing…" She stopped in the middle of her sentence and got real close to the brick. A thin line had been cut into the wall all the way around the brick. She tried pushing on the brick. Nothing happened. She pushed harder. Still nothing. Nugget was staring at the brick with his eyes squinted and tail wagging. Leila sat on the ground, scooched Nugget out of the way and kicked the brick as hard as she could.

CRACK!

It broke free, revealing a small hole in the wall. Inside the hole was a package.

THE OCEAN BLUE

Nugget stopped dead in his tracks. Leila carefully pulled the package out of the wall and unwrapped it. Inside were a dozen 70-year-old chocolate bars. Leila picked up one of the bars and turned it over in her hand. The wrapper said "Bobo Bar! Fresh and Delicious!"

Mrs. Crenshaw's face lit up. "A Bobo Bar!" she said. "I haven't seen one of those for 50 years!"

"What is it?"

"They were supposed to be the freshest chocolate bars because they used a red, see-through inside wrapper instead of the usual silver paper. I don't think the red wrapper did anything special to keep the chocolate fresh, but it made me believe Bobo Bars were the best, so they always seemed to taste a little better."

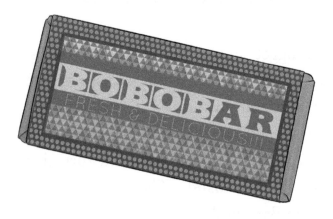

"I don't think it's fresh anymore," Leila said, noticing the expiration date was September, 1949.

"Try opening it," Mrs. Crenshaw said. "Maybe there's a clue inside."

Leila made a face.

"Go ahead," Mrs. Crenshaw said. "It's just chocolate. It's not going to stink."

Leila held her nose just in case and carefully unpeeled the outside wrapper. Nothing but red plastic and an old candy bar inside. "I don't get it," Leila said. "Does this mean…" Leila stopped in the middle of her sentence when she took a second glance at the outside wrapper. There was writing underneath. Leila's eyes got huge as she read the message.

Good job by you,
You've found clue number two!
Here's a treat
For you to eat
As you solve the mystery.
In 1492,

Columbus sailed the ocean BLUE.
But what would it mean
If the sea were GREEN?
Would it really change the things you've READ?

Leila turned to Mrs. Crenshaw with the biggest grin on her face. "It's a clue! A real clue to a real treasure hunt! Eeee!"

Mrs. Crenshaw couldn't contain a little smile of her own. "Let's put the rest of these candy bars back into the wall and get out of here before my nephew sics the dog catcher on us.

Mrs. Crenshaw drove Leila home, and the two of them stayed in the car for 30 extra minutes trying to figure out the riddle. That night, Leila took twice as long as usual to finish her homework because her mind kept going back to the poem. On top of all her excitement about the clue, there was a little nervousness that she wouldn't figure it out in time. After all, there were only a few short months left in the school year.

The next day at school, Leila tried to concentrate. She really did. But no matter how hard she tried, she couldn't focus on the War of 1812 when all she wanted the teacher to talk about was Christopher Columbus. Things didn't get any better at lunch.

"…afraid of the tree?"

Leila looked over. Kait was staring at her like she was expecting an answer to a question. "What did you say?" Leila asked.

Kait huffed. "Why was the cat afraid of the tree?" she repeated.

Leila gave her a weird look. "Why would you ask me that?"

"It's the riddle on my Laffy Taffy!" Kait held up an empty wrapper. "I ask you my Laffy Taffy riddle every day! What's wrong with you?"

"I'm sorry," Leila said. "I've just had a lot on my mind lately."

"It's like I'm talking to a zombie,"

Kait said. She tapped Leila on the head a few times. "You're not a zombie, are you?"

"Don't be a weirdo," Leila said. Zombie. Was that a clue? Zombies are green, right?

"You sure there's nothing you want to tell me, Ms. Zombie?" Kait asked.

"Uh, no." Leila felt bad about fibbing to her friend, but she'd just come up with an idea. She needed to visit the library.

Kait looked at her with squinty eyes for a second, then said, "Because of its bark."

"Huh?"

"Because of its bark. That's the answer to the riddle."

Leila still looked confused. "Oh."

Kait threw her head back and yelled her frustration to the ceiling. "Unnnnnng!"

Leila looked at the clock and stood up. "Sorry, Kait. I've got to do something real quick."

"Probably eat some brains, right?!" Kait shouted after her. "Nice, juicy brains!"

Leila shook her head as she walked out the door. She just needed a few minutes to check out every Christopher Columbus book the school library had. Leila was convinced there was something she needed to learn about him to solve the riddle. At the library, she was disappointed to find that there was only one book about Christopher Columbus, and it was a thin one for little kids. "I'm sorry," the librarian said. "We just don't have many books like that anymore. Have you tried the Internet?"

Leila sighed, nodded and thanked the librarian. Then the bell rang, and she hurried to art class. Between the library and the art classroom was the music room. Leila's heart pounded faster as she neared it. The music room would always be her own secret spot — the place where she…

Leila suddenly stopped breathing and stopped walking. She put on the brakes so fast that the person walking behind her bumped into her back. The brick was gone, and the hiding spot was wide open. Leila ran over and bent down to look inside.

It was empty.

5

BOBO BARS

Leila started panicking. Who could have found the spot so fast? She didn't remember seeing another person in the whole school yesterday afternoon. Had someone been watching her? Wait, was someone watching now?! Leila popped her head up and looked at everyone walking by. Amelia? Did Amelia just give her a weird look? Why was Chase digging in his bookbag like that? What was he trying to hide? Leila spent the rest of the day trying to figure out who'd discovered her secret.

After school, Leila clipped the leash onto Nugget and loudly announced, "I'm going for a walk with the dog! Nothing special!" You know, just in case someone had put spy cameras into her house. Can't be too careful. Leila took 20 minutes to walk to Mrs. Crenshaw's house, zigging and zagging and spinning in circles the whole way. Nugget, of course, loved it. When she was sure that nobody had followed her, Leila walked up the driveway to her friend Javy Martinez's house, then cut through his backyard into Mrs. Crenshaw's yard. She snuck to her back door and knocked while looking over her shoulder.

Mrs. Crenshaw seemed surprised to see Leila at the wrong door. "What are you..." she started to ask before Leila ducked underneath her arm into the house. Mrs. Crenshaw closed the door and turned around with her arms crossed. "What's going on?" she asked.

Leila had wide eyes. When she opened her mouth, a bunch of words spilled out in a jumble. "A spy! There's a spy, and he's following me, and I don't know where he's at, and I don't know if he put cameras in my house, or..." At that moment, Leila's eyes got even bigger, which seemed impossible because they were already really wide, "…or your house! We need to look for cameras right now! They could be listening to us!" Leila started looking all around the ceiling like a crazy person.

Mrs. Crenshaw snapped her fingers in Leila's face. "Hey! Hey!" That got Leila's attention. "Stop talking nonsense. There are no cameras."

"But, but…" Leila was almost in tears by now. "But someone else found the second clue!"

"And?" Mrs. Crenshaw asked.

"And, well, isn't that bad?"

"No, it's not bad, and it certainly doesn't mean there's a spy," Mrs. Crenshaw said. "This isn't the movies. There aren't spies hiding cameras to win an elementary school scavenger hunt. As a detective, you've got to learn that the simplest answers are usually the right ones. Now, what's the simplest answer?"

"That someone hid a camera and…"

"Wrong," Mrs. Crenshaw interrupted. "The simplest answer is that my nephew saw you digging in the wall yesterday and took the weird bag of old candy bars to the office."

"Oh," Leila said, suddenly feeling a little silly. "I guess that makes sense."

"And even if another student happened to find the clue, so what? This is a treasure hunt! Treasure hunts are supposed to have competition."

Leila sure didn't want any competition, but if Mrs. Crenshaw was right, then she was still the only one who'd seen the clue. She started to feel better.

That is, until lunch the next day.

"Oh brother," Kait said, shaking her

head at her Laffy Taffy. "This is a grandpa joke."

"A grandpa joke?" Leila asked, her mouth full of apple.

"Yeah, a joke my grandpa would tell me when I was little. It's that old. Don't they pay someone there to write jokes? That's the job I want when I get older."

"Well, what is it?" Leila asked.

"What's black and white and red all over?" Kait read, rolling her eyes. "So lame."

"Black and white and red?" Leila hadn't heard that one before. "Wait don't tell me. I can figure it out."

"Sooooooo lame," Kait repeated.

"Is it like a zebra with…" Leila stopped in the middle of her answer because something across the cafeteria caught her attention. It was an older boy stuffing his face with a chocolate bar.

Next to his hands, crumpled in a ball was the unmistakable, clear red wrapper of a Bobo Bar.

Leila immediately stood up and started marching across the cafeteria. She'd found her spy, and she had a LOT of questions to ask him. The boy was much bigger than her, and she didn't know exactly what she'd say, but she wasn't about to let him get away with this. "Excuse me," she said when she arrived.

All the eyes at the table turned to Leila. "Uh, can I help you?" the boy asked.

Leila held out her finger like a lawyer pointing at the bad guy in court. "Where did you get that?"

The boy looked confused. "This? Did she try to sell you one too?"

Now it was Leila's turn to be confused. "Did who try to sell me one?"

"It's actually pretty gross," the kid said. "She acted like it was some rare candy that was going to be the best thing I'd ever tasted, so I gave her two dollars for it. Two whole dollars for a single candy bar! That was dumb. Don't let her trick you too."

"Let who trick me?" Leila asked. "Who sold that to you?"

The boy scanned the cafeteria, then finally found the candy dealer. "There," he said.

Leila spun around. He was pointing at Kait.

6
NEWSPAPER

When Leila made it back to the table, Kait was ready for her. "So you figured it out, huh detective?"

"Why would you spy on your best friend?" Leila asked.

"Why would you hide something from your best friend?" Kait shot back.

"I wasn't hiding it from you. I just wasn't telling you."

Kait blinked a few times. "That literally makes no sense."

Leila sighed. "How did you do it?"

Kait smiled a smug, little smile. "Well, you were clearly up to something the other day, so I got on my bike and followed you to that old lady's house."

"You know her name is Mrs. Crenshaw."

"Right, OK. So anyways, I waited outside for a few minutes, then just as I was about to give up and go back home, you guys got in the car. It looked like you were heading toward the school, so I biked there. When I finally got to the school, the janitor wouldn't let me in, but he told me that you went to the music room. The next day, I found the weird brick outside the music room, pulled it back and voila." Kait made a fancy motion with her hand and bowed.

"So you decided to sell the candy bars?"

"No," Kait said. "I decided to eat them. To get back at you. But they were gross, so then I decided to sell them."

"They were 70 years old," Leila said.

Kait made a face and turned a little green. "I did not know that."

"So you didn't care about the treasure?" Leila asked.

Kait looked at Leila out of the corner of her eye. "What treasure?"

"Do you have any of the candy bars with you now?" Leila asked.

Kait dug one out of her backpack. Leila peeled back the outside wrapper and showed her the riddle. Kait gasped. "What does that mean?!"

Leila told Kait everything about Principal McGee, the 70-year-old treasure and the president in the picture. It felt great to finally share things with her best friend again.

By the time she finished, Kait was exploding with questions. "So there's a buried treasure right here in the school?!"

Leila shrugged. "Probably."

"And nobody knows what it is?!"

"Nope."

"So it could be gold or something?!"

"I mean, probably not."

"Yeah. It's a treasure. It's definitely gold. And you didn't tell me about this gold — why, again?"

Leila sighed. "Because you have a tough time keeping secrets, and I didn't want the whole school to know about it."

Kait gasped and made a face like Leila had just hit her. "You wanted the treasure for yourself!"

"That's not it at all!" Leila said. "I was going to tell you! I mean, I just didn't think you could…"

"I wouldn't have told anyone," Kait said. "You know why? Because you're my friend. And friends keep secrets for each other. But I guess that's not as important to you as some dumb treasure." With that, Kait got up and stomped away, leaving her lunch behind.

"Kait! Come on, Kait!" Leila shouted after her friend. She started picking up Kait's stuff to take back to her. Was Kait right? Should Leila have shared her secret earlier? Leila was deep in thought when she picked up Kait's Laffy Taffy wrapper and noticed the answer to the joke Kait had been trying to tell her earlier. "A newspaper."

A newspaper? Even though Leila had a thousand things on her mind, the answer made her stop. That didn't make sense. Newspapers are black and white, but they sure aren't red. Leila turned the wrapper over and read the joke for herself. "What's black and white and read all over." Ohhhhh, now Leila understood. A newspaper is READ all over the place; it's not the color red. Funny. Well, not really funny, but funny in a grandpa joke kind of way. She crumpled the garbage and then cleaned the rest of Kait's mess. But as she was putting the Bobo Bar back into Kait's backpack, the candy bar's clear, red inside wrapper caught her eye. Leila held the Bobo Bar to her face.

"Of course! That's it!" she said to herself.

"Did you figure out the candy bar clue?" someone asked.

Leila's head shot up. Gwyneth Watson from Mrs. Liggins's third-grade class was sitting at the next table, holding up her own Bobo Bar. "We've been trying to figure it out all lunch," Gwyneth said. "What do you think it means?"

Leila's heart started pounding. How many people were now looking for the treasure? She had to find Kait.

7

RUNNING SHOES

Leila ran into Kait pacing angrily in the hallway. "Kait!" she said as she handed over the bookbag. "How many of those candy bars did you sell? I think I figured it out, but we need to hurry because..." Kait pretended that she didn't hear Leila and walked away in the middle of her sentence.

During science class, Leila tried to get Kait's attention with Kait's favorite thing: a note. But when Kait opened the note and saw who it was from, she crumpled it up. On the bus, Leila tried to sit next to Kait, but Kait had already taken the seat next to Javy.

When Leila got home, she immediately plopped on her bed and started talking to Nugget. "Errrrg, this is so frustrating!"

Nugget laid next to her and put his head on her lap.

"I mean, I finally figure out the second clue, but I would feel bad about going on until I make things right with Kait, you know?"

Nugget gave Leila's hand a little lick. He knew.

"I know I should have told her before; I just didn't want her to blab it to the whole school. But guess what? She somehow ended up blabbing anyways! So now, who knows if Kait will ever forgive me? And while I'm worrying about that, someone else might find the clue before I do! Should I just look for the clue now?

Do you think Kait would understand?"

Nugget rolled over for a tummy rub. Leila started scratching. Nugget wiggled around until he found a cozy spot, then lay there with his eyes closed and tongue half hanging out of his mouth. Leila sighed. "Yeah, I know."

Leila got a few things together, walked to Kait's house and knocked on the door. Kait's mom answered. "Hi, Leila!" Then she looked down at Nugget, puzzled. "What's this?"

"Hi, Mrs. Korver. It's a message for Kait. Can I talk to her?"

"Kait!" Mrs. Korver yelled. "Nugget has a message for you!"

"Can't come to the door!" Leila heard Kait yell from upstairs. "I'm busy!"

Mrs. Korver shook her head. "Hold on," she muttered to Leila as she turned around and walked upstairs. A minute later, she returned, holding Kait by the arm.

"What?!" Kait asked.

"Look." Her mom pointed.

Nugget was staring back at Kait with giant puppy eyes and a sign around his neck that said, "I'm sorry."

"So?" Kait asked.

"So you listen to her," Mrs. Korver said. "You don't ignore someone who's trying to apologize." Kait sighed, and her mom left.

"I'm sorry," Leila said.

"OK."

"No, I mean it. I had this secret, and I wanted it for myself. It felt special, ya know? But friends share stuff with each other, especially secrets. You're my best friend, Kait, and I should have shared this secret with you. I understand why you would feel hurt. Do you forgive me?"

Kait folded her arms across her chest. Nugget looked up and wagged his tail harder.

"Also," Leila added. "I think I figured out the riddle, and I was wondering if you'd help me look for the next clue."

Kait was trying to play it cool, but she

couldn't stop her eyes from lighting up. "You figured it out?"

Leila nodded. "But you didn't answer my question. Do you forgive me?"

"Of course I forgive you," Kait said. "You were probably right anyways. I mean, I do like to blab. Now tell me what the clue means!"

Leila smiled. "Well, first, we're going to have to go to Mrs. Crenshaw's house."

Kait made a face. Leila knew that Kait didn't like Mrs. Crenshaw because Mrs. Crenshaw had yelled at her a few years ago. "Unnnnnng," Kait said.

Ten minutes later, Leila, Kait and Nugget were walking to Mrs. Crenshaw's house. They would have left earlier, but Kait had insisted on finding her fastest running shoes in case Mrs. Crenshaw tried throwing her in a pot of boiling water and she needed to run away. When they reached the house, Mrs. Crenshaw opened the door and welcomed Kait by holding out her hand. "Hello there, I'm Mrs. Crenshaw."

Kait paused, then shook her hand. "Kait Korver," she said. "Uh, how do you do?" Kait wasn't normally the type of kid who goes around asking people, "How do you do," it just seemed like the right thing to say to people Mrs. Crenshaw's age based on Kait's experience with black-and-white movies.

"Korver, huh?" Mrs. Crenshaw said. "Hm, interesting."

"Interesting?" Kait asked, alarmed. "Why is that..."

"I think I figured out the clue!" Leila blurted. She'd been keeping this inside for far too long, and she couldn't bear to hold it in any longer. She walked to the kitchen and took off her jacket. As she walked, she kept talking. "What's black and white and red all over?"

"A newspaper," Mrs. Crenshaw and Kait answered at the same time. "It's the oldest joke in the world," Kait added.

"Right," Leila said. "It's a good joke to tell someone else, because 'read' and 'red' are easy to confuse when you hear them."

"OK," Kait said. "So?"

"Remember the clue? 'Columbus sailed the ocean BLUE. What would it mean if the sea were GREEN.' The two colors were capitalized in the poem. Then I realized the third capitalized word might also be a color." She pulled the Bobo Bar out of her pocket and pointed to the inside wrapper.

"Ohhhh," Kait said. "It's red!"

"Would it change the things you've READ!" Leila said. "This red wrapper is the key to figuring out the next clue!"

"I don't get it," Kait said.

"The poem makes it sound like the red color would change things. That made me think of those spy lens codes they sometimes have on cereal boxes. Do you know what I'm talking about?"

Kait shook her head.

"The back of the cereal box will have a jumble of shapes and numbers that don't look like anything. But if you cover the picture with the 'spy lens' you find inside of the box, you can see through the mess, and a secret code appears. Well, the spy lens is just a colored piece of plastic like the Bobo Bar wrapper. So if this is a spy lens code, we need to put the red wrapper over a map of the ocean that Christopher Columbus crossed!"

Mrs. Crenshaw started clapping. "That's brilliant!" she said.

"But what map?" Kait asked. "Any

map in the school from 70 years ago has to be gone by now, right?"

"Gone from the school," Mrs. Crenshaw said. "But maybe not gone altogether." She disappeared into the living room.

"See?" Leila said. "She doesn't bite."

"That's what she wants you to think while she figures out a way to kidnap us," Kait said.

Mrs. Crenshaw returned a minute later. "Put your jackets back on, girls. We're going to find this map."

Kait's eyes got wide. Leila laughed. "Come on, Kait, it's OK." Kait shook her head and backed up, ready to use her running shoes. Leila looked back at Mrs. Crenshaw. "Maybe it would help if you told us where we were going."

Mrs. Crenshaw smiled at Kait. "We're going to your grandmother's house."

158

8

THE ZOO

In the car, Mrs. Crenshaw explained why they were visiting Kait's grandma. "Kait, your grandmother and I have become quite close over the last few years because we both share the same interest — books."

Kait made a face at Leila in the back seat. Books were definitely *not* one of her interests.

"A few years ago in one of our book clubs, I mentioned a book I'd remembered from my childhood — *Happy Birthday, Mr. Tortoise*. It was the first pop-up book I'd ever seen, and I remember that it felt like magic. I spent hours as a child opening and closing the pages to figure out all the folds that made the pop-up pictures work. Well, the next week in book club, your grandmother gave me that exact book! It was 75 years old, and some of the pictures had been ripped, but your grandma had taped everything back together, so it was almost as good as new. She said she'd found the book in her attic. Kait, did you know your grandma was the school librarian for 40 years?"

"Mmhmm," Kait said. "It's all she ever wants to talk about."

"When the school got rid of old books, your grandma would get to take them home with her. She has quite a collection in the attic."

"Oh, I know," Kait said. "When I was little, my cousins and I would build huge forts up there with all the books until my grandma found out and made us stop."

"There's one book in particular that I asked her to look for. I hope she has it."

When they arrived, Kait's grandpa opened the door. "Pumpkin!" he said when he saw Kait.

"Poppy!" Kait gave him a hug. Then she noticed the old Scottish Terrier at her grandpa's feet. "Hey, Baxter!"

The dog gave her a little tail wag, then his eyes got big when he saw Nugget bound toward the door. Nugget ran up to the elderly dog and jumped around him for a full minute while Baxter waited patiently.

Kait's grandma came down the stairs holding the biggest book Leila had ever seen. "Hi, Kait, hi, Margie," she said. She gave Mrs. Crenshaw an air kiss on both cheeks. "I found the atlas you wanted."

"That book is humongopotamus!" Leila exclaimed.

Mrs. Crenshaw nodded. "I think it was the biggest book at the school for a long time, right Judy?"

"You're probably right," Mrs. Korver said. "I remember Principal McGee was so proud of it. It came from his personal collection."

Everyone gathered around the old book as Kait's grandma carefully opened it and started turning pages. Each page had a giant map of a country, complete with hand-drawn details and fancy lettering. Mrs. Crenshaw broke the silence. "I remember going to the library sometimes after school just to flip through this atlas and imagine traveling to the countries inside."

Kait made a face. "You read a book of maps?"

"Life was pretty exciting back then, huh?"

"There's something special about these kinds of books though," Mrs. Korver said. "It's too bad the school library can't buy them anymore. It just got too expensive, especially since students could find everything they needed online. Still, nothing's quite the same as getting lost in a big, old book like this."

They kept turning pages until they got to a full spread of the Atlantic Ocean. Leila got a tingling in her tummy as she pulled out the candy bar wrapper. "Let's see what we've got!" Everyone huddled around while Leila carefully slid the wrapper over the page. Nothing popped out.

"Try it again," Mrs. Crenshaw whispered.

Leila did. Nothing. She sighed. "Maybe it's on a different…"

"THERE!" Kait squealed.

Leila looked down. "I don't see anything."

"That dragon thing! Go back to that dragon thing!" Kait was so excited that she was jumping up and down.

Leila slid the wrapper back down to the corner of the page. There it was! Hidden in the tail of a big, red sea monster was a small set of numbers and letters written in green — 736.98. "Wow, Kait! You're a genius!"

Kait was grinning ear to ear. "A rich genius! We're getting $736.98!"

"That's not money, dear," Kait's grandma said. "It's a Dewey Decimal number."

Kait's grin turned into a frown. "Oh. Uh, what's that? Is it like money?"

Now it was Mrs. Korver's turn to frown. "The Dewey Decimal System? It's the number system used to organize books in the library."

Kait stared blankly at her grandma. "Oh."

Mrs. Korver groaned. "Where did I go wrong? In the Dewey Decimal System, the 700s are all books about art, and the 730s all have to do with sculpting. Now a book numbered 736.98 would be about..." Mrs. Korver looked at the ceiling for a moment. "Paper folding and origami."

Everyone stared at Mrs. Korver with their mouths hanging open. Even the dogs. "You just knew that?" Kait asked. "Off the top of your head?"

Mrs. Korver winked. "I was a librarian for a long time."

"So you think the next clue is in a book about origami?" Leila asked.

"There's only one way to find out!" Mrs. Korver said as she gleefully led everyone to the attic. Once they'd all reached the top of the creaky stairs, Mrs. Korver clicked on a single lightbulb. Leila gasped. It looked like every book that had ever been written was stuffed in the attic. Bookcases, shelves, bins, boxes — all overflowing with old books. "How will we ever find it?!" Leila asked.

"What kind of librarian would I be if I didn't sort this all by the Dewey Decimal System?" Mrs. Korver replied.

Sure enough, less than a minute later, they'd found the only origami book in the attic and started flipping through it. Kait used the Bobo Bar wrapper to look for another hidden clue. Leila searched for suspicious writing. Mrs. Korver inspected the check-out card. Nobody found anything until Mrs. Crenshaw made a suggestion.

"You don't think he used the bookmark secret, do you?"

Mrs. Korver's eyes lit up. "Kait, can you get a butter knife from the kitchen?"

"What's a bookmark secret?" Leila asked as Kait ran downstairs.

"When we were in school, the students had this little game where we would pass notes to each other by hiding bookmarks in the binding of big books. We all thought we'd kept it a secret from the adults, but Mr. McGee was smart.

He knew all of our tricks."

Kait returned with a butter knife, and Mrs. Korver carefully slid it down the spine of the book. "I think I hit something!" she said. Everyone leaned in as she pushed the knife farther and farther until a yellow piece of paper peeked out of the bottom.

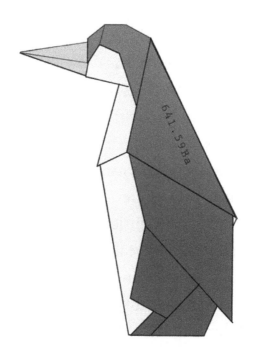

"Eeeps!" Kait squeaked.

Mrs. Korver pulled the paper all the way out and held it up. It was a beautifully folded paper penguin with another Dewey Decimal number written on its wing. Kait squeaked again. "Where's this one?!" she asked.

"Should be a cookbook," Mrs. Korver replied.

Five minutes later, Mrs. Korver pulled a paper elephant from the spine of an old book called, *The Handy Cookery*. That elephant had another Dewey Decimal number on it that led them to a turtle in a history book, which led them to a snail in an astronomy book. Written on the snail was another poem. Mrs. Korver read it aloud for everyone.

You've completed your zoo,
Onto the final clue!
If you're brave and strong,
You won't be wrong —
Just climb up, up and away.

Mrs. Korver set the snail down and smiled at everyone. "I know where it is."

9

THE FINAL CLUE

Leila and Kait were the first ones off the bus when it pulled up to school the next day. "Let's go, let's go, let's go!" Kait yelled as she ran inside.

Leila shushed her. "Right now, we're the only ones who know about this. We've got to keep quiet to make sure nobody gets to the treasure before us. Got it?"

Kait nodded, made a lip-zipping motion and turned into the gymnasium. Leila followed her. Inside the gym, Leila pulled her dad's big binoculars out of her bookbag and started scanning the rafters.

"See anything?" Kait asked.

Leila shook her head. "Your grandma said it was in the middle of…"

"Hey!" A voice interrupted them. "You girls need to get to class!"

Leila gulped. It was Mr. Glaser, the P.E. teacher. Mr. Glaser was the scariest teacher in school. He wasn't exactly mean, but he did kind of act like he was running an Army boot camp most of the time in gym class. Plus, he used to be a football player, and even though that was a long time ago, he was still really big and muscley. Kait did the talking.

"Hi, Mr. Glaser," Kait said. "We're looking for the rope."

"The what?"

"The rope!" Kait repeated. "Ya know, the one that went all the way up to the ceiling."

Mrs. Korver had told the girls about a

big rope that used to be in the gymnasium. Students would have to climb all the way to the top for P.E. class. Both her and Mrs. Crenshaw agreed that it was the worst thing they ever had to do in school. "Strong and brave, climb up, up and away…" The clue must have been talking about the rope.

Mr. Glaser looked confused. "The school cut that down 20 years ago."

"We know. We're just trying to figure out where it was tied. Do you remember?"

"I wasn't even the P.E. teacher then."

"But you went to school here, right?" Kait asked. "Can you remember where it was when you were a kid?"

Mr. Glaser's patience was wearing thin. "Are you going to tell me what this is about?"

"A treasure," Kait said matter-of-factly.

"OK, you two really need to get to class."

Kait crossed her arms. "And you really need to return The Secret of Wildcat Swamp."

Mr. Glaser squinted at her.

"Thaaaaat's right," Kait said. "The Secret of Wildcat Swamp. Hardy Boys Book #31. You checked it out from the school library on November 3, 1984, and you haven't returned it yet. Even if we go by the 1984 fine rate of five cents per day, you owe $620.50. You've been running from the law for a long time, mister, and my grandma sent me in to collect. Of course, she's willing to forget about the fine if you help us find the clue."

Mr. Glaser rolled his eyes. "What is it?" he asked — not so much because he was afraid of paying an old library fine, but because the girls didn't seem to be going anywhere until they got their answer. Leila explained the treasure hunt and the clue as fast as she could.

Mr. Glaser looked skeptical. "So you think there was some sort of treasure clue at the top of the climbing rope?" The girls nodded. "I've got to tell you," Mr. Glaser said, "I climbed up there a bunch of times when I was a kid, and I never saw anything."

"Can you just look?" Leila pleaded. "It would make us really happy."

"And it would make you happy to not have to pay a $600 library fine. Mwahahaha!" Kait added.

"I'll look up there," Mr. Glaser said. "But only because your grandma was always nice to me." Mr. Glaser disappeared into the equipment room

175

and re-emerged a few seconds later pushing the Mover-Matic, an elevator platform he used to hang banners from the rafters and retrieve balls that had gotten stuck.

"See that hook thing up there?" he asked, pointing to the ceiling. "That's where the rope was." He locked the Mover-Matic into place and climbed onto the platform.

Kait's eyes got big. "Do you think…"

"Absolutely no kids allowed on the Mover-Matic!" Mr.

Glaser said as he pressed a button and started rising in the air.

"Worth a try," Kait whispered to Leila.

Once Mr. Glaser made it up to the hook, he took a few seconds to look around. "Definitely no clue," he finally said. "I'm coming back!"

"Wait!" Leila yelled. "Keep looking! What else is around the hook?"

"Six tons of steel beams," he said. "I'm coming down." The platform started moving back down.

But Mr. Glaser did a funny thing after he pressed the down button. He quickly ran his hand over the steel beam. Even though he said he didn't believe in the treasure, even though he was giving up, even though he acted like Leila and Kait were silly for making him do this, there still must have been a tiny part of him that wanted to believe something was up there.

"Whoa." Mr. Glaser said after he felt the beam. He stopped the platform.

"What is it?!" Leila yelled.

Instead of answering, Mr. Glaser moved the platform back up to get a better look. He got real close, then peeled something off the top of the beam. "I don't believe it!" he said. "It looks like a note!"

The girls jumped up and down and met Mr. Glaser when the Mover-Matic finally reached the floor. "Thank you! Thank you so much!" Leila said.

Mr. Glaser shook his head. "I wouldn't have believed it if I hadn't seen it with my own eyes," he said as he handed the yellowed piece of paper over to Leila. Leila carefully unfolded it and read it aloud.

Use your herd
To guess the magic word.
Then tell it to the man
Where it all began,
And the treasure will be yours!

The three of them were silent for a second. Finally, Kait asked, "What does it mean?"

"Yeah, what do you think it means?" a voice behind Kait repeated.

Oh no. Leila recognized the voice. It was Gwyneth Watson — the same girl who'd been trying to figure out the Bobo Bar clue the day before. She must have noticed Leila and Kait running off the bus and followed them to the gymnasium. With all the excitement of the final clue, Leila hadn't noticed her. Maybe she could convince Gwyneth to keep this little secret for just a bit longer.

Leila started to turn. "Hi, Gwyn…"

She froze. Behind Gwyneth, waiting eagerly for her response, was half the school.

10
PINECONES

And just like that, Leila's secret, little treasure hunt had become the opposite of secret and little. Anyone who hadn't seen the final clue with their own eyes had heard all about it within an hour. By lunchtime, the whole school was searching for treasure — even some of the teachers! And if that weren't bad enough, Channel 5 News had gotten wind of the 70-year-old treasure, and they came to the school with cameras and everything.

Leila felt sick. She walked Nugget around the block three times after school that day, fuming the whole time. "It's not fair!" she said to Nugget.

He responded by sniffing a tree.

"After all that hard work, now someone else is going to find my treasure."

Nugget picked up a pinecone with his mouth, looked back at Leila and tried to sprint ahead. He quickly dropped it, though, when he ran out of leash.

"Unnng. Do you think there's still a chance?"

Nugget picked the pinecone back up and zigzagged for the next few minutes to keep Leila from stealing it. Leila barely noticed. She'd made up her mind.

"I'm going to find that treasure first because I'm going to work harder than everyone else."

And she did work harder than everyone else. Leila thought about the

case every spare second of every day —
even some non-spare seconds while she
was supposed to be listening in class.
Every day, she had a new clue to add to
her notebook. Every afternoon, she had a
new idea to share with Nugget on their
walk. And every walk, Nugget had a new
pinecone to steal.

Leila quickly discovered that she had
two big problems. One was that she had
no idea what the "magic word" was. She
figured it must have something to do
with the origami animals because the clue
mentioned "the herd." But no matter
how long Leila spent staring at the
animals or how many times she unfolded
them, she couldn't figure out the magic
word. Then, there was the bigger
problem that "the man where it all
began" had been gone for 70 years. Even
if Leila did figure out the magic word,

she couldn't tell it to Mr. McGee. So what was the point?

The point was Leila had come this far, and she wasn't giving up now. So she kept looking and thinking and digging every day. Of course, she wasn't alone. The week following the discovery of the final clue was a full-blown treasure frenzy. Treasure clubs formed during lunch, hunting expeditions set out during recess and teachers even canceled some of their classes so students could look for the treasure together. Although Leila was worried about all the new people looking for the treasure, she took comfort in knowing that none of them had the origami collection. She swore Kait to secrecy — neither of them could breathe a word about the animals to anyone. It was their only hope of figuring out the final clue first.

She didn't need to worry, though. Nobody even got close to finding the treasure. Soon, Leila was the only one looking again. The idea of a treasure right beneath your feet is fun, but actually searching the school and puzzling over clues for hours on end? No thanks. Even Kait, who'd been so excited to strike it rich in the early days, got bored. Every time Leila started discussing possible clues with her, Kait would try to turn the conversation back to what they'd do with all the money. She'd start talking about buying a five-pound gummy bear, then she'd wonder how much real-life CIA spy equipment costs, then she'd start rambling about her dream treehouse until Leila would finally give up on the conversation and go home.

Weeks and months went by. Now

every time Leila passed the new school building, she got sad instead of excited. The beautiful windows in front and the giant playground in back were reminders that the clock was ticking on her treasure. The worst moment came during the last week of school. After turning in the final math test of the year, Leila plopped back in her seat, breathed a sigh of relief and looked out the window to daydream. That's when the sigh turned into a groan. Right next to Mrs. Pierce's third-grade classroom was parked a giant, yellow bulldozer.

That day after school, Leila hung her head during her whole walk with Nugget. "This is it," she said. "Summer vacation starts tomorrow, and then the treasure will be gone for good."

Leila sounded so sad that Nugget stopped sniffing long enough to come back and nuzzle her.

Leila smiled and bent over to pet him. "Thanks, little buddy."

Nugget let her scratch him for a few seconds before galloping off again.

"I just thought for sure I'd find it," Leila continued. "Like for sure, for sure. I never even cared if it was gold or money or anything. I just wanted to know what it was! That's the worst part. Now nobody will know what it is."

Just then, Nugget started sprinting. He'd found the pinecone tree. He grabbed the biggest one of the bunch, then ran ahead like normal. But this time, after just a few steps, he stopped. Instead of zigging and zagging and trying to keep the pinecone away from Leila, he turned around, walked back to her and set the pinecone at her feet.

"Awwww!" Leila put her hand over

her mouth. "That's the sweetest thing ever, Nugget! That was so nice of you to share!"

Nugget started wagging his tail. Leila picked up the pinecone and stared at it for a minute. Suddenly, she knew what she needed to do.

I PLEDGE ALLEGIANCE

"Attention!" Leila said when she stepped on the school bus the next day. "Attention, everyone!"

A few sleepy eyes looked her way.

"I want to invite everyone to join together and help me search for the Englewood Elementary treasure today! We are stronger together than we are apart! Together, I believe…"

"Leila," Miss Carol said without turning around. "Can you please sit down so I can start driving?"

"Oh, uh, of course," Leila said.

As soon as she could, Leila got Kait

and Gwyneth Watson to help her gather a group of kids together to share everything she knew about the treasure. She told them about President Harrison, the secret in the map — she even brought out the origami animals.

"Wait," Gwyneth said as she turned the paper turtle over in her hands. "You had these the whole time, and you didn't tell anyone?"

"I didn't either!" Kait said, proud of herself for not blabbing this big secret.

"I really wanted to be the one to find the treasure," Leila said. "But I realize now that I was just being silly. Every clue I found came because someone helped me. Mrs. Crenshaw, Kait, Mr. Glaser — even my dog! So now I'm sharing this with all of you and asking for your help. Would you guys help me figure out the magic word?"

Everyone was on board. Mrs. Pierce's third-grade class was supposed to have an end-of-the-year party that day, but most of the juice and donuts went untouched because the entire class was working on the case. By ten o'clock, they'd organized into a code-cracking unit. Kait was at the front of the class with the pointer, tapping animal names on the board. "Penguin, Elephant, Turtle, Snail. What do those four animals have in common? They all have four legs, obviously, so…"

"Penguins and snails don't," someone interrupted.

"They all have four legs, EXCEPT FOR PENGUINS AND SNAILS, I was going to say," Kait said. "So that's suspicious. Also, all four animals have been to outer space, I think."

Students looked at each other, confused. "What if the paper animals come to life when you put them in a certain spot in the school?" one of the kids suggested.

"Have you tried burning them?" someone else asked. "Maybe there'll be a clue in the smoke."

People started shouting half-baked ideas over each other until the room was complete craziness. Kait looked at Leila, threw up her hands and walked to her seat. Leila shook her head. It was a good try. She got up and walked toward the donut table. On her way, she passed Benjamin Balmer, the quietest kid in class. Without a word, Ben stood up, walked to the front of the classroom, picked up a piece of chalk and underlined the first letter of every animal — Penguin, Elephant, Turtle, Snail. Then he wrote the letters in order at the bottom of the chalkboard.

P-E-T-S.

Then he sat back down.

The room went silent. Leila stared with her mouth open. That had to be it. After all those months, she couldn't believe she hadn't thought to do that. "Uh, wow. Thank you, Ben. I think you just figured out the magic word," Leila said.

The room burst into applause.

Ben was a hero for about five minutes until everyone realized that they didn't know what to do with the code word. With Principal McGee gone, what good did it do? The class tried chanting, "Pets! Pets! Pets!" a few times, until Mrs. Pierce made them stop.

After she'd quieted everyone down, Mrs. Pierce spoke to the class. "I'm proud of you all for working together to solve this mystery," she said. "Although it didn't lead to an actual treasure chest, you all discovered the treasure of teamwork today, and that's worth all the gold in the world. Why don't you give yourselves a hand?"

The class halfheartedly clapped. The treasure of teamwork? Yuck.

Mrs. Pierce smiled and continued. "It's almost noon, so let's clean up and head to the flagpole for the Final Pledge. Then it's off to summer vacation!"

Leila sighed as she threw away her trash and took her place in line. For her, the treasure hunt was always more about figuring out the mystery than finding a bunch of gold. And they'd solved the mystery, right? So why wasn't she more excited? Kait patted her on the back. "You did great," she said.

When Mrs. Pierce's class walked outside and saw the scene at the flagpole, they all said, "Whoooooooooaaaaaa," at once. It looked like half the town was there. For as long as anyone could remember, it'd been Englewood Elementary's tradition for the students to gather on the last day of school for one final Pledge of Allegiance. With this being the last day for the old school, a bunch of extra people had joined the tradition this year. Parents, grandparents and people who'd graduated decades earlier had all come together to say goodbye to the old building. Mrs. Crenshaw was there, Kait's grandma was there, even the Channel 5 News crew had returned for the big occasion.

Principal Brown stepped in front of the crowd. "Wow," she said. "This is incredible. I know this place holds a special place in all of your hearts. As sad as we are to see it go, we are just as excited to make brand new memories in our new building this fall. Now, will you all join me as we salute the flag for one final Pledge of Allegiance."

Everyone put their hand over their heart and pledged as one.

"I pledge allegiance to the flag of the United States of America, and to the Republic, for which it stands…"

Kait looked around while she pledged. All the kids had giant grins on their faces as they tried to speed up the pledge so they could start summer break two seconds faster.

"…One nation, under God…"

A lot of the adults looked sad. One or two even had watery eyes. Leila could tell the moment was bringing them back to their childhoods, when this simple tradition marked the beginning of a three-month adventure away from school.

"…Indivisible…"

Wait a second. *Where it all began.* Leila's mind snapped back to the mystery, and her palms started sweating. She may have just figured out the whole thing.

"…With liberty and justice for all."

All the students cheered.

"Thank you so much!" Principal Brown said over the commotion. "Have a safe summer!"

As the crowd dispersed, the janitor, Mr. Peterman, walked to the flagpole to take down the flag. Leila quickly followed after him. "Excuse me, Mr. Peterman?" she said.

He turned around. "Yes?"

Leila's heart was beating out of her chest. "Pets."

Mr. Peterman stared at her for a second, then a big smile spread across his face. He walked to the platform that Principal Brown had been speaking from and got everyone's attention. "Excuse me!

Excuse me, everyone! I have one more announcement." He pulled Leila onto the platform with him and held up her arm. "This young lady just claimed a 70-year-old treasure!"

TREASURE WHEREVER YOU GO

One voice squealed above the noise of all the confused people.

"AHHHHH!"

It was Kait.

"AHHHHH! This is so exciting! AHHHHH!"

Kait pushed her way to the front of the crowd to hug Leila. "ARE YOU RICH NOW WHERE IS IT WHAT IS IT WHAT HAPPENED?!"

Leila smiled. "Seeing everyone here for the Pledge of Allegiance today made me think of a line from the last clue. 'Tell it to the man where it all began.' Remember?"

"Of course," Kait said. By this time, Kait's grandma and Mrs. Crenshaw had also made their way to Leila.

"We always thought that part was talking about Principal McGee because he was the one who began the treasure hunt. But that's not what the poem says. It says '*WHERE* it all began.' So it's talking about a place. And where was the treasure hunt supposed to have begun?"

"The flagpole!" Mrs. Crenshaw said.

"Exactly! So you're not supposed to tell the magic word to Mr. McGee, you're supposed to tell it to a man who will be at the flagpole. And since it's the last day of school, that man is going to be the one in charge of taking down the flag after the Pledge."

Mr. Peterman wiggled his eyebrows.

"Let me tell you all something that you're not going to believe," he said as he flipped through his keychain. "When you become the Englewood Elementary janitor, you get two things from the old janitor: a set of keys and instructions to unlock a cover at the bottom of the flagpole if — and only if — a student comes to you with the code word, 'Pets.' I always assumed that second part was a joke until that clue came out a few months ago."

"I can't believe you never told me!" Mrs. Crenshaw said.

"I'm sworn to secrecy, Aunt Margaret!" Mr. Peterman said. "It's the Janitor's Code! Anyways, all that time went by with nobody claiming the treasure, so I just figured that it would be lost forever. Now, I can't wait to see what it is!"

Mr. Peterman finally found the right key, knelt at the flagpole and wiped off some dirt to reveal a small lock. By this time, dozens of people had crowded around the scene, including one of the news cameras. "Do you want to do the honors?" Mr. Peterman asked Leila when he pushed the key into place.

Leila grinned and turned the key. She expected it to be hard to turn since the lock hadn't moved in 70 years, but it clicked right into place. Leila opened the cover, reached into the compartment and pulled out a musty burlap sack.

"How much gold?! How much gold?!" Kait asked, trying to get a better view over Leila's shoulder.

"It's not that heavy," Leila said.

"Even better! Paper money!" Kait exclaimed.

Leila reached into the sack, and

everyone leaned in closer. "It's... it's..." she grabbed a stack of something and pulled it out. "Baseball cards?"

"Baseball cards?!" Kait exclaimed. "BASEBALL CARDS?!"

"I mean, they're pretty old baseball cards, so that's cool," Leila said as she pulled out more packs.

"That's not a treasure!" Kait said.

Leila reached back into the bag. "Wait, there's a box in here too!" Everyone leaned forward again as Leila pulled it out. "Oh, cool!" Leila said when she saw what it was. "It's an old doll!"

The Channel 5 cameraman sighed and lowered his camera. Real treasure would have been so great for TV ratings.

"Looks like there's a note taped to the back of the doll," Mrs. Crenshaw pointed out.

Leila opened it up. "It's one last note

from Principal McGee!" she said.

The Channel 5 guy turned on his camera again.

Leila cleared her throat and read it aloud for the crowd.

You did it! You found the treasure!
Baseball cards for him and a doll for her.
Now keep discovering! Continue learning!
Be growing, stay yearning,
And you'll surely find treasures wherever you go.

"I don't get it," Kait said. "Does that mean there are like baseball cards and dolls all over the place?!"

Leila shrugged. "I don't know. The best part of this treasure hunt wasn't the stuff at the end; it was all the cool clues hidden in plain sight. Maybe that's what Principal McGee was trying to say — if you keep your eyes open, you'll start finding awesome stuff all around you. What do you think, Mrs. Crenshaw?"

"I think you've figured it out again, detective."

Kait slumped her shoulders. "That's cool, I guess. I just think a mountain of money would have been cooler."

"Don't give up on that money mountain just yet," Mr. Peterman interrupted. He was holding the baseball cards. "These are 1940 Play Ball cards. They're really rare, especially in perfect condition like this. This set had Ted Williams, Joe DiMaggio, Shoeless Joe Jackson — if you find a couple of the good cards in these packs, you're looking at a few thousand dollars easy!"

Kait gasped. "You are rich! I'm friends with a rich lady! What are you going to do with all the money?!"

Leila thought about it for a moment. "Well, I don't really feel like it's my money," she finally said. "It kind of seems like it belongs to you and your grandma and Mrs. Crenshaw and our whole class for helping me with the clues. I wish there were a way I could share it with everyone."

"What about candy?!" Kait said. "You could give candy to everyone! Or maybe buy us all a TV or a pony or..."

"Books!" Leila interrupted.

"What?"

"Books! That's it! That's exactly the type of treasure Principal McGee was talking about!" Leila said. "Our school library isn't what it used to be, but we can fill it back up with all kinds of cool books for kids! What do you think about that, Mrs. Korver?"

Kait's grandma squeezed Leila. "I

think that's wonderful, honey! Just wonderful!"

Kait looked up in the air. "Uggggh! Why do I have to be friends with such a nerd?!"

"Hey, I think we can keep a few dollars to buy something fun for us."

"Like what?"

Leila smiled and gave her own clue. "What's an animal that's chewy and gooey?"

"An animal that's chewy?" Kait gasped. "A gummy bear?!"

Leila started walking away.

Kait followed close behind. "A five-pound gummy bear?! Please tell me it's a five-pound gummy bear!"

leila & nugget
MYSTERY
#3
bark at the park
deserae & dustin brady

BIG DOG

"Excuse me! Sorry. Whoops! Nugget, slow down!" Third-grader Leila Beal struggled to pull back her little dog, Nugget, as he sprinted ahead.

"Just let the little guy enjoy himself," Leila's friend, Kait, said.

"I would, but he's tangling everyone up in his leash!"

Nugget couldn't help it. He'd never

seen so many new friends in his life. Leila and Kait had joined over 200 people and their dogs, all decked out in Middleburg Red Dogs gear, inside their town's minor league baseball stadium. Today was the Red Dogs' eighth annual "Bark at the Park" game, where fans were allowed to bring their dogs to the ballpark. While the special day had started as a fun, little promotion, it'd quickly grown to become one of the town's biggest traditions. The coolest part of Bark at the Park was always the Pup Parade around the bases to start the game. Then there were special treats and activities for the dogs throughout the afternoon. Finally, after the baseball game was over, the Middleburg Dog of the Year would be crowned.

This was Leila's first-ever Bark at the Park, and she couldn't have been more excited about it. To celebrate, she'd even made Nugget his own Red Dogs hat with a little strap. Of course, he wasn't wearing it now because he'd freaked out once she'd put it on his head, but Leila still brought it to the game just in case. She'd also convinced Kait to bring her grandparents' old Scottish Terrier, Baxter. Baxter was not amused.

"It's OK, Bax," Kait said to the grumbling, little dog. "We're gonna do the parade soon, then we can eat snacks for the rest of the afternoon!"

As if on cue, a woman in a suit walked on top of the dugout and tried to get all of the dog owners' attention. "Thank you for coming, everyone!" she yelled over the barking. She waited until the dogs quieted down to continue. "This might be our biggest Bark at the Park yet! I'm going to ask you all to follow me underneath the stadium. We'll be a little cramped for a second, but don't worry—Big Dog will be right there to lead us onto the field for the Pup Parade. OK, let's go!" The woman climbed back down and unlocked a door next to the dugout.

Leila, Kait and their dogs followed the crowd through the door. They walked down a few stairs and entered an old hallway that smelled like moldy laundry. The woman was right—it was super cramped. This hallway was made for players to get to the clubhouse, not 200 dogs to squish into.

Baxter started whining. Kait picked him up. "I know, little buddy. I don't like crowds either." She turned to Leila. "What are we waiting for? Some big dog?"

"No, not a big dog. Big Dog. The mascot."

216

Kait wrinkled her nose. "A big, red dog? You mean Clifford?"

"No. It's just 'Big Dog.' Also, they don't like people calling him 'Clifford.' I think they might have gotten sued once."

Kait still looked confused.

"Haven't you ever been to a Red Dogs game before?" Leila asked. "Big Dog is a cartoon mascot that walks around, giving high fives and throwing t-shirts. Also, he judges the hot dog race."

"OK, there's no such thing as a hot dog race at a baseball game."

"No, it's this thing they do at Red Dogs games now where three hot dog mascots race around the bases. It's the best part of the game. The last time I was here, Big Dog took the onion hot dog's hand and got down on one knee like he was asking her to marry him. He's really funny."

"Well he'd better get here quick because Baxter is about to lose it," Kait said.

Leila nodded. Now that she thought about it, it was kind of amazing that all these dogs were behaving so well despite being packed so close together. While they waited for Big Dog, Leila kept herself busy by trying to identify all the

218

different breeds of dogs in the hallway. A kid she recognized from school was petting a fluffy, yellow dog. Golden retriever. Easy. Next to him was a dog big enough to ride on. Leila guessed that one was a Great Dane. Across from the Great Dane, a teenage girl held a purse with a little, pointy-eared dog sticking out of it. Definitely a chihuahua. Then next to the teenager...

Leila elbowed Kait. "Hey!"

"What?"

"Isn't that Jenny Jones from Mrs. Liggins's class? What's she doing here?"

Kait took a break from comforting Baxter to look up. "Yeah, that's Jenny. She's probably walking in the parade. What's wrong with that?"

"Nothing, except she always talks about how much she hates dogs, right? Doesn't she only like cats or something?

219

Plus, she's not even holding a leash—she only has that bookbag."

"She's probably just got a little dog in there or..." Kait got distracted halfway through her answer by Baxter trying to squirm out of her arms. "Hey, come on!"

Suit Lady got everyone's attention again. This time, she had to really yell since the dogs sounded much louder in the small hallway. "I'm sorry Big Dog's not here yet!" she said. "He was supposed to be waiting for us. I'm going to find him. Everyone stay put for just a minute longer."

Kait turned to Leila with a worried expression. "Wait, where is she going?! It's so hot down here! Are you hot? I feel like I can't breathe!"

"It's OK," Leila said. "Just breathe. We'll be out of here in a minute."

Kait wasn't the only one starting to

panic. Many of the dogs had begun to bark and howl. Others were pawing at each other. The Great Dane had begun sniffing Jenny Jones's bookbag suspiciously.

"I can't breathe!" Kait said, holding her throat. "It's so smelly!"

The Great Dane was now poking the bag with his snout. Jenny noticed and tried to move, but that only made the dog poke harder. Suddenly, a head popped out of the bookbag.

It was a cat.

The Great Dane's eyes got wide. The cat's eyes got wide. Every dog in the hallway turned to the intruder. For a moment, everything was silent.

Then, the place erupted.

2

CAT'S OUT OF THE BAG

"Are you sure you're all OK?" Leila's dad asked for the third time.

Leila nodded. Five minutes after escaping the hallway, her ears were still ringing, but at least they worked. "Yeah, Dad. It was just a little scary for a second."

"THAT WAS MORE THAN A LITTLE SCARY!" Kait shouted a bit too loudly, probably because her ears were ringing too.

Kait was right—for a few moments, nothing in the world was scarier than that hallway. As soon as the dogs realized that a cat was in their presence, they all went bonkers. The sound of 200 dogs barking at once bounced around the small hallway, which made the dogs even crazier. Several of them escaped from their owners and started a stampede. Fortunately, Jenny was standing near the end of the hallway, so she was able to escape before any of the dogs got her cat. Unfortunately, her end of the hallway happened to be the one near the field. Jenny sprinted onto the field with two dozen dogs following her, their owners chasing after the leashes. Even now, five minutes later, a few dogs were still running wild in the outfield.

Kait and Leila had joined the crowd running back to the stands. It was a tight squeeze, but they'd all made it. With all the scared people and dogs trying to get through the same door at the same time, it was a small miracle that everyone seemed to be fine. In fact, Nugget was more than fine—he looked ready to do it again.

"Well, that was an adventure," Leila's dad said. "You girls get your things together, and we'll head home."

"But, Dad! What about the Pup Parade?"

Leila's dad pointed to a guy tripping over second base as he chased a poodle through the infield. "At this point, they'll be lucky to get the game in. They're not doing the parade."

"Please, can we just wait another few minutes? At least until the hot dog race!"

"That's not until the sixth inning," Mr. Beal said. "Look, I know it's a bummer. I was looking forward to watching the game too. But..."

"Oh, look! Let's ask her!" Kait

interrupted, pointing to the suit lady from earlier. "Excuse me!" she said. The woman looked her way. She had dirt on both knees, and some of her hair was sticking straight up. "Do you know if we're still going to do the Pup Parade?"

"Yes!" the lady said. "Wait, no. I don't know, probably not. Have any of you seen Big Dog?"

"No, is he missing?" Kait asked.

"Yes! That's why all this is happening! We couldn't find Big Dog, and then the dogs just snapped."

"So if we find Big Dog, we can do the parade?" Leila asked hopefully.

The lady looked over Leila's shoulders and pointed. "There he is!"

Leila turned around, expecting to see a giant, red dog. Instead, it was a skinny college kid with worried eyes. "Mrs. Gilmore!" he said.

"Nick! What happened? Where's the costume?!"

"Mrs. Gilmore, I'm so sorry. I can't find it anywhere!"

"What do you mean you can't find it? I handed it to you this morning."

"I know! And then I hung it up in the mascot closet. When I came back, it was gone!"

"Are you sure you didn't forget where you put it?"

"Yeah! It's not an easy thing to misplace."

"Nick! You know how important that costume is! If you didn't misplace it, then what happened?"

"Mrs. Gilmore," Nick looked around and leaned in. "I think someone stole it!"

"Who would..."

"We're on the case!" Kait shouted.

3

PUPPY PALS

Both Nick and Mrs. Gilmore whipped their heads around. They didn't realize the girls had been listening the whole time.

"The what?" Mrs. Gilmore asked.

"The case!" Kait said. "We're on the case! Leila here is a professional detective, and my name is Kait. I'm her sidekick."

"That's very nice, girls. But I don't think you can help."

"You ever heard of the Englewood Elementary treasure?" Kait asked. "Leila's the one who found it. No big deal."

"Uh, no, I haven't heard of that,"

Mrs. Gilmore said.

"That was you?!" Nick asked. "I saw that on the news! That's so cool!"

Leila blushed. "I had a lot of help."

Mrs. Gilmore's radio crackled. "Stacey, can you get us some help on the field? This dog's too fast!"

"I'll do that now," she said into the walkie-talkie. Then she looked at Nick. "I need you to find that costume. It's expensive, and Mr. Gilmore has had it for a long time."

"I understand," Nick said.

"Now if these girls think they can help, take them with you."

"Oh, no," Nick said. "That won't be necessary."

The radio crackled again. "Two more dogs just jumped onto the field! What do we do?!"

"Coming!" Mrs. Gilmore said into the

radio. She turned back to Nick. "Looks like I'm going to be running around all day. If they can't help find the costume, at least they can watch the puppies." Then she walked away before Nick could protest.

Puppies?! The girls turned to Leila's dad. "Pleeeeaaaase?!"

"You still have the emergency phone Mom gave you, right?" he asked Leila.

"Of course!" Leila dug the flip phone out of her pocket.

"OK. But stay with an adult."

"Hooray!" Kait spun around with Baxter. He was not amused.

"Come with me," Nick grumbled.

The girls followed Nick back underneath the stadium and turned into a small room off the main hallway. When Nick opened the door, a blast of air conditioning hit the girls.

"Brrr!" Kait wrapped her arms around her body. "Are you guys using this room as a freezer? Why... AWWWWWWW!"

Kait forgot all about the temperature when she spotted a blanket in the corner of the room bundling a litter of the cutest puppies ever. "They're adorable!" Kait said. "What kind are they?"

"I don't know," Nick replied. "They're Mrs. Gilmore's. I think they're Labs or something."

Nugget bounded to the puppies and started sniffing and licking like crazy.

"Can I hold one of them?" Kait asked.

"Sure. You two keep an eye on these guys while I try to find the costume," Nick said, walking out the door.

"Eeee!" Kait squealed as she ran toward the puppies.

"Wait!" Leila grabbed her shoulder. "We're here to solve a mystery, remember?"

Kait rolled her eyes. Nick did too. "Look," he said. "It's very nice of you to offer, but this is my problem. I've got this."

Leila stood her ground. "Since the parade got canceled because of this, it's our problem too. If we find the costume before the end of the game, maybe we can save the parade." She took out her notebook. "Can you tell us everything you know about the missing costume? Has this ever happened before?"

Nick sighed. The girls didn't look like they were going anywhere. "Fine. I don't know if the costume has ever been stolen before because this is the first time I've ever been Big Dog. Mrs. Gilmore's husband usually does it. He's been Big Dog for almost 20 years."

"Why are you doing it today?"

"He just had knee surgery," Nick said. "That's why the puppies are here too. He can't take care of them by himself at home, so Mrs. Gilmore's watching them here. Anyways, my mom is friends with Mrs. Gilmore, and she volunteered me to be Big Dog for the summer. Looks like I lost the job after one day."

"So how long was the costume out of your sight?"

"Not long. Maybe 15 minutes. I hung it up over there when I left the room around 11," Nick pointed to a coat rack with an empty hanger. "And when I came back, it was gone."

Leila wrote that down in her notebook, then looked around for clues. The room was pretty empty—there was the coat rack, a tall mirror, a coffee pot, a refrigerator, a few chairs and...

Leila picked up a wallet from one of the chairs. "Is this yours?" she asked.

Nick's eyes got big. "I can't believe I left that out!"

This wasn't adding up. A thief walked past a wallet lying out in the open? Leila looked back at the puppies. There were four of them. "Are any puppies missing?"

Nick shrugged. "I can't remember how many there were."

"Oh, I have an idea!" Kait piped up. "We can check the security cameras!"

"I don't think they have any in here," Nick said.

"Can we check? Oh, please, please, please?!" Kait loved spying on people, so a room full of camera screens was a dream come true for her.

"I saw a room that said 'Security' down the hall," Leila offered.

"We can't just leave the puppies," Nick said.

Leila looked back. Nugget and Baxter had curled up next to their new friends. Baxter was already asleep, and Nugget was still licking their blanket.

"Nugget!" Leila said.

He looked up with his tongue half-sticking out of his mouth.

"Stop it!"

He stuck his tongue back in and laid his head on top of one of the puppies.

"Our dogs will keep them safe," Kait said. "Now let's go!"

Kait led the way to the security room.

One wall of the room had six TV screens, all with 16 different camera feeds going at once. "This is great!" Kait said. "Let's try to find Leila's dad!"

"Kait!" Leila complained. "Focus!"

"Right," Kait sat and started scanning screens. "What are we looking for?"

"Anything suspicious," Leila said.

"OK!" Kait edged closer to the screens and squinted. "That guy looks a little too excited to be at a baseball game. Baseball is boring. And she's typing something on her phone. Can we zoom in to see what she's typing? Oh, that guy is dressed up just like one of the players! That's weird!"

"He is one of the players," Nick said.

"OK. Less weird. WHOA!"

"What is it?" Leila asked.

"Big Dog! I saw him!"

"Where?!"

"Over there!" Kait pointed to a screen showing dozens of people walking by a row of concession stands.

"Are you sure you saw the costume?" Nick asked.

"Of course! Yeah, I'm pretty sure. I mean, probably."

Leila and Nick gave each other skeptical looks.

"How do you rewind?" Kait asked.

"I don't know!" Nick said. "This is my first day on the job! I don't think we're even allowed in here!"

Nick got up to leave, but Leila grabbed his arm. "There!" she said. "We need to go there!"

She pointed to a screen showing another small room underneath the stadium. Sitting in a chair in the middle of the room was Jenny Jones, the girl who'd started the stampede.

CATS RULE

"Jenny? You think it was Jenny?!" Kait asked as they hurried down the hall.

"Keep your voice down," Leila said. "I don't know, but it kind of makes sense."

"You'll have to explain that to me before we accuse this girl," Nick said.

"Whoever stole the costume passed up your wallet," Leila said. "So they probably weren't interested in the money they could make by selling the costume, right?"

"I guess."

"Then what did they want? There aren't many things you can do with a six-foot-tall mascot costume. What if they were trying to ruin Bark at the Park?"

"I don't get it," Nick said.

But Kait did. "Oh wow! Jenny loves making dogs look dumb!"

Leila nodded. "What if she hid the costume so we couldn't start the parade, then she brought out her cat when all the dogs were squished together to make them go crazy?"

"Whoaaaaaaaa," Kait said. "What an evil supervillain plan! She's basically the Joker!"

Nick wasn't buying it. "OK, maybe she's the Joker, or maybe—just maybe— she's a scared kid who thought it was pet day at the ballpark instead of just dog day. What do you think is more likely?"

When he put it that way, Leila thought that maybe her idea sounded a bit silly. But before she could answer,

Kait piped up. "Joker. Definitely the Joker." She looked through the window in the door to her left and saw Jenny holding her cat. "This it?" she asked.

Nick nodded as he opened the door. "Just let me do the talking, OK?" he said.

"Mom!" Jenny yelled when she saw the door begin to open. "I was so scared! I..." she stopped when she saw Leila, Kait and Nick instead of her mom.

"Scared of what?" Kait asked. "Scared someone would figure out your evil plan? Well, guess what? We already did!"

"Evil plan?! What are you talking about? Where's my mom?"

"Your mom can't save you now!" Kait said with her finger in the air.

Nick grabbed Kait's finger and shoved it down. "I'm so sorry," he said to Jenny. "This was such a bad idea. We were just going."

"Wait," Leila said. "Hey, Jenny. Sorry about all this. Big Dog's missing, and we're just trying to help Nick find it. Do you think you could help us?"

Jenny held her cat closer. "Why would I help you find a big dog? Fifi almost got killed by a big dog earlier!"

"That must have been so scary for you," Leila said.

"It was! I knew Fifi was scared in that tunnel full of dogs, but she was being so brave and quiet, and that dumb dog decided to go after her anyways."

242

"Oh, don't you blame this on the dogs!" Kait yelled. "You were the one…"

Leila elbowed Kait. "What made you bring Fifi into that tunnel in the first place?" she asked.

Jenny put her nose in the air. "Cuz cats are better than dogs."

"Excuse me?" Kait said, squinting and leaning in close.

"You heard me." Jenny squinted back. "Cats. Are. Better. And even though everyone knows they're better, cats aren't allowed at the baseball game. Ever!" She looked at Nick. "Why is there no Meow at the Park? Huh? Why not?"

Nick put up his hands. "Don't look at me! This is my first day!"

"Just because you like cats doesn't mean you have to ruin dog day for everyone else," Kait said.

"Ruin it? I was just trying to show

that cats could do Bark at the Park too! Even better than dogs!"

"You really should have left the cat at home," Nick said. "That was dangerous."

"Yeah," Jenny shot back. "You know why? Cuz dogs are dumb."

Leila was just about to give up when she noticed Jenny's bookbag. Even though she'd taken the cat out of it, it still looked full. "I'm glad that you and your cat are safe," Leila said. "Last thing so we can go—can you open your bookbag real quick?"

"What?" Jenny asked. "No. Why do you need to see inside my bookbag?"

Kait noticed how big the bookbag was too and gasped. "Cuz you've got a Big Dog costume in there!"

Jenny shook her head hard. "No way, Jose!"

"If you just open it real quick, we'll

244

leave you alone," Leila pleaded.

"Listen, I saw some big, dumb mascot walking around earlier," Jenny said. "It was by the bleachers or something. Why don't you go check it out?"

"Just open your bookbag!" Kait said as she started unzipping the bag herself. "What are you trying to hide?!"

"Nothing!" Jenny yanked the bag back so hard that it unzipped all the way, and poster board flung across the room. The sign landed face-up on the floor so everyone could see its message—CATS RULE! DOGS DROOL!

Kait folded her arms. "Oh, but you weren't trying to ruin Bark at the Park. You just wanted to bring your little, innocent cat."

Jenny stuck her nose in the air. "I'm not saying another word until my mom gets here."

"Fine!" Kait said.

"FINE!" Jenny said.

"HA! That's another word!"

"We're leaving," Nick said. "NOW."

Kait started whining as they walked out of the room. "We got her, though! She was trying to ruin Bark at the Park!"

"We didn't get anyone," Leila sighed. "She didn't have the costume."

"Then she must have hidden it somewhere!" Kait said as she opened the door to the mascot room. "We'll find it if it's the last thing we..."

Kait gasped. There was Baxter, standing at the door with his tail wagging. There was Nugget, still sniffing and licking. And then next to Nugget were three cute, little puppies.

One was missing.

NO DOGS ALLOWED

"Baxter! Where did the puppy go?!" Kait yelled.

Baxter heard the word, "go," and perked up. He really wanted to go.

"Oh, this is bad," Nick said. "This is really, really bad. Losing the costume is one thing. But losing a puppy? I'm dead."

"Back to the security room!" Leila said. "If we hurry, we might be able to spot it!"

Nugget raced back to the security room with Leila, Kait and Nick. Leila started scanning the video feeds as soon as she stepped inside. "Kait, take those screens! Nick, you look over there!" Leila focused on the screens showing the bleachers. So many people! She pulled Nugget up to take a look. He was great at spotting dogs.

"No kids in the security office!" an angry female voice commanded from the doorway. Leila spun around in her spinny chair to apologize. Before she could even turn all the way around, the woman noticed Nugget and gasped. "NO DOGS IN THE SECURITY OFFICE!"

"You're the one with the dog!" Kait yelled back.

When Leila finally turned all the way around, she discovered what Kait meant. The yelling voice belonged to a stern security officer holding Mrs. Gilmore's missing puppy. The woman had a nametag on her chest that said, "Franklin."

"I'm allowed to have this dog! I belong here. You know who doesn't belong here? All ya'll!"

"Oh no," Leila said. "She just meant that we were looking for that puppy, and we're happy you found it!"

"Found it? It was never lost!"

"Oh, because we didn't see it..."

"I fed it, if that's what you mean.

They told me some kid named Rick was supposed to take care of these dogs."

"You mean Nick?" Nick asked, sheepishly raising his hand.

"You Nick?" Officer Franklin asked.

Nick nodded.

She handed him the puppy. "They've got me feeding puppies, watching kids, chasing dogs. They don't pay me enough for this."

"I'm sorry, ma'am," Leila said. "I was supposed to watch the puppies with my friend, Kait, while Nick looked for a mascot costume that may have been stolen. Have you seen it?"

"The dog one?"

"That's right."

"No," Officer Franklin said. "It's usually hanging up in the mascot room next to my uniform. It wasn't there today. When did it go missing?"

250

Leila looked at her notebook. "He walked out of the room for 15 minutes around—what time did you say, Nick? Like 11 a.m.?"

Nick suddenly looked uncomfortable. "I don't know. It's hard to remember."

"Yeah, it was 11," Officer Franklin said. "You were leaving just as I was getting here. Remember?"

"Ohhhhhhh, uh, yeah, I guess," Nick said.

"Well all the costumes were gone by then," Officer Franklin said.

Leila looked up from her notebook. "What?"

"My uniform was the only thing on the rack when I got here. He must have misremembered."

"Do you think we could look at the tape from the security camera?" Leila asked.

"There aren't any cameras in that room," Officer Franklin said. "People get dressed in there."

"OK, well maybe we could look at the video from the hallway to see who else might have gone in that room?"

Officer Franklin's radio squawked. "Can we get security to section 106? A loose beagle won't leave the hot dog guy alone."

Officer Franklin huffed. "One thing after another. Listen, I can try to help you later, OK?" She shook her head as she left the office. Then she yelled back, "I meant what I said earlier! You kids get out of my office!"

Leila, Kait and Nick hurried back to the mascot room. Once inside, Nugget licked the puppies again. He was happy to see his new friends. Leila closed the door and turned to Nick with her arms folded across her chest. "OK. Spill it."

"Spill what?" Nick asked.

"You know what!" Kait said, even though she clearly didn't know herself.

"Why did you fib about when the costume went missing?" Leila asked.

"I didn't fib! I misremembered!" Nick said, even though he was making a guilty face.

Kait lit up. She'd been waiting to interrogate someone all day. "Spill it, pal! Or I'll sic my vicious dog on you!" She pointed at Baxter, who was trying to curl up and get comfy. Baxter sighed.

Nick looked around the room. "I'll tell you guys, but you have to promise not to tell Mrs. Gilmore."

6

JUICY RED

"How about we call Mrs. Gilmore right this second?" Kait said.

"And tell her what? I didn't steal anything!" Nick insisted.

Kait pointed to Leila, who pulled the emergency phone out of her pocket. Kait grabbed the phone and started punching in a random number. "Hope she believes that because we've got two witnesses in this room who heard you confess. Actually, eight if you count the dogs."

Nick looked nervous again. "Put that away!" he said. "I told you, I didn't steal the costume! But..." he looked around again and lowered his voice. "I wasn't completely honest."

Kait hovered her finger above the send button and looked at Nick with her eyebrows raised in a "tell me more" kind of way.

Nick sighed. "Mrs. Gilmore has spent the last week reminding me over and over how much that costume means to her husband. She has a bunch of rules for wearing it – rules that would be impossible for anyone to follow."

"Like what?" Leila asked.

"Like no sweating in the costume, even though it's basically a head-to-toe coat you're wearing in the middle of the summer. I mean, it's made of fleece. Fleece!"

"How did she expect you not to sweat?"

"I was supposed to come back to this

room and cool down every time I got hot throughout the game. That's why they keep the air conditioning blasting so cold. But even then, I'm gonna sweat. It'd be impossible not to!"

"OK, that is kind of crazy," Kait admitted. "What other rules did she have?"

"No running in the costume, no dancing on top of the dugout, check all hands for nacho cheese before giving high fives. But the craziest one is no drinking pop while wearing the costume."

"Why is that so crazy?" Leila asked.

Nick motioned to the refrigerator in the corner. "Being a mascot is hard work, so the Red Dogs keep a refrigerator stocked with all sorts of drinks."

Kait opened the fridge. "Whoa! They have everything in here! Fancy bottled

water, Gatorade, iced tea. Wait, is that..."
She dug into the back of the fridge.
"JUICY RED!"

"Exactly," Nick said. "And that's why
the 'no drinking in the costume' rule is
the most impossible."

"I don't get it," Leila said, examining
the Juicy Red can.

"You'd understand if you tasted it!"
Kait said.

Leila opened the pop and took a sip.
It was super-duper sweet. Like if

someone figured out how to turn cotton candy into a fizzy drink. "Pretty good."

"Pretty good? Pretty good?!" Kait asked with wide eyes. "It's the best thing ever! And you can't buy it anywhere! They stopped making it like two years ago!" She turned to Nick. "How did you get this?!"

"I guess Mr. Gilmore loves it, so the Red Dogs bought him a huge supply before the company went out of business. Anyways, I noticed the Juicy Red this morning after I'd already put on the costume. I couldn't believe it—Juicy Red is my favorite drink of all time! Obviously, I had to take a sip."

"Obviously," Kait agreed.

"As soon as I started drinking, one of the puppies tugged on my leg. I knew I wasn't supposed to be drinking, so that little tug startled me so much that I spilled Juicy Red all over the inside of the costume."

Leila looked back down at the pop. It was almost neon red. "That must be Mrs. Gilmore's worst nightmare."

"Exactly," Nick said. "As soon as it happened, I turned the costume inside out and tried to wash it with the bottled water. When that didn't work, I ran to the laundry room where they clean the players' uniforms to see if they had anything for the stain. So instead of hanging it back in the closet, I draped it inside out over that chair to let it dry. When I came back, it was gone!"

"And you don't have any idea who might have taken it?"

"For a while, I figured it was that security lady trying to get me in trouble with Mrs. Gilmore. But she hasn't said anything yet, so it's probably not her."

Nick leaned in closer. "I think someone's using it for blackmail."

"That makes sense," Kait said. "Wait, what's blackmail?"

"When someone knows a secret you're trying to keep, they can threaten to tell everyone to make you pay money," Nick said.

"Oh, well I know how we can fix this," Leila said.

"How?"

"We just tell Mrs. Gilmore what happened."

"What?!" Nick yelled. "No! Didn't you hear anything I just said! That's exactly what we don't need to do!"

"But if she knows, then the blackmail won't work. Plus, the pop will come out in the wash. Mrs. Gilmore might be mad for a little bit, but she'll understand."

"Nope, nope, nope. No way."

At that moment, the door opened, and a head popped in. "It's the fourth inning, and all the dogs are under control," Mrs. Gilmore said. "Please tell me you found my husband's costume."

SUPER-DUPER FIRED

"Go home. You're fired."

"But, Mrs. Gilmore..." Nick protested.

"You're fired," Mrs. Gilmore repeated. Her arms were folded. After she'd walked into the room, Leila, Kait and Nick had danced around the truth for awhile before Kait finally spilled it. "How could you not be fired?!" Mrs. Gilmore asked. "You ruined my husband's costume and then lost it before you even started your first day!"

"I'm sorry. I shouldn't have drunk pop while wearing the costume."

"My husband loves Juicy Red! LOVES it! And in 20 years, he's never drunk it in the costume! You know why? Because he takes care of his stuff!"

Leila stepped up. "Mrs. Gilmore, I know you're upset."

"I'm furious!"

"But the thief probably won't leave the stadium until the game's over, right?"

"Hmf."

"So maybe you could unfire Nick for a little bit so he can help find the costume before it gets away for good."

Mrs. Gilmore thought about it for a second. "You are temporarily unfired," she finally said. "But after this game, you're super-duper fired. Understood?"

"Yes, ma'am."

Without another word, Mrs. Gilmore stomped out and slammed the door.

Nick turned to the girls. "You happy now? I knew that would happen!"

"Maybe we can still get your job back," Leila said.

"How?!"

"You figure out how to get Juicy Red out of clothes. We'll search the stadium for the costume thief."

"You're never going to find it," Nick said with his head in his hands. "The stadium's too big."

Leila and Kait clipped their leashes onto their dogs. "Don't worry," Leila said. "We're going to recruit some help." She scooped up one of the puppies and smiled. "Everyone loves a puppy!"

Kait grinned and picked one up too. "Puppies are the best!"

Leila gave Nick the number to the emergency phone in case he found anything and marched back out of the tunnel with Kait. The girls blinked a couple times when the sunlight hit their faces. "I actually kind of don't get it," Kait said. "What are we doing with the puppies?"

"Follow my lead," Leila said as she fitted Nugget's Red Dogs hat onto the puppy.

Just then, the girls heard an "awwwwwwwww" to their left. They turned to see the chihuahua owner from the tunnel. She was pointing to the puppies. "They're sooooo cute!" She elbowed her friend with an Australian Shepherd. "Look!" She turned to Leila and Kait. "Can we pet them?"

"Of course!" Leila said. Soon, several more dog owners had gathered around. When the crowd got big enough, Leila told them about Big Dog. "Have any of you seen anything suspicious?" she asked.

"It's that Clifford dog, right?" Chihuahua girl turned to her friend. "Didn't we see him earlier?"

Her friend shrugged. "Maybe by home plate?"

Leila and Kait thanked the group then started walking toward home plate. They got ten steps before...

"AWWWWW!"

Another large group gathered around the girls. This group hadn't seen anything, but they all agreed to keep an eye out. One of the boys had a German Shepherd who'd been trained to find things with his nose. Give the dog a sniff of Juicy Red, and he'd find the costume in no time, the boy promised. Ten seconds after they left the German Shepherd, the girls got stopped again. This time, they met a girl cavapoo named Penelope that looked just like Nugget. Nugget immediately fell in love. The two dogs started playing and got their leashes hopelessly tangled in seconds. Penelope's owner promised to walk her dog all the way around the stadium to look for Big Dog.

By the sixth inning, Leila had snapped 20 pictures of Nugget with his new doggy friends, Kait had to borrow treats from 12 different people to keep Baxter moving and half the stadium had volunteered to search for Big Dog.

"Nobody knows anything, and Baxter might explode if he eats one more treat," Kait finally said. "Do you have any other ideas?"

"The costume was underneath the stadium, so the person who took it probably works for the team," Leila said. "Asking the fans is good because it gives us more eyes to help look, but if we're going to find the costume, we're going to have to go places most fans can't."

"How are we going to do that?" Kait asked.

Leila smiled and walked to the "Krazy Kettle Korn" concession stand. "Excuse me," she said. "Do you happen to have a water bowl for my puppy?"

The woman at the counter smiled at the puppy. "Oooo, you thirsty? You a thirsty puppy?" Then she looked back up at Leila. "No problem, come back here!" Inside the concession stand, the woman gave the puppies some water and Nugget and Baxter some popcorn. While she did, Leila and Kait took a quick look around. Nothing suspicious. The girls tried the same thing at Nacho Heaven with the same results.

When they got to Big Dog's Chili Dogs, Leila got a text. "Do you have any vinegar?" she asked the cashier after looking at her phone.

"We do if you buy fries."

"Oh. Hey, look at my puppy!"

The cashier put her hand over her mouth. "Oh my gosh, that is the cutest puppy I've ever seen!"

After every worker at Big Dog's Chili

Dogs petted the puppy, Leila got her free vinegar after all.

"Why do you need that?" Kait asked.

Leila shrugged and pointed to the press box. "Let's look in there." When the two girls and four dogs marched into the press box, the reporters all looked alarmed. They looked even more alarmed when Leila asked her question. "Do any of you have newspaper for my puppies? I think they have to go to the bathroom."

While the reporters all scrambled to find paper, Kait snooped in every drawer and cubby hole for any sign of a costume. Nothing. The girls didn't give up. After the press box, they found ways to get into the video booth, the scoreboard operator's room and the umpire lounge. Still nothing.

Leila sighed as she plopped onto a bench. "That's it. I'm all out of ideas. I thought for sure we'd find something."

"Don't feel bad," Kait said. "You did your best. Do you want to break the news to Nick, or should I?"

"We can in a second. I want to rest first." Leila pulled out her phone and started scrolling through pictures. There were some really cute dogs. She especially liked the beagle and the one that looked like a fox and Nugget's girlfriend... "Whoa!" Leila said when she got to Penelope's picture. "Look at this!"

Kait squinted at the picture. "What? I don't see anything. Can you make it bigger?" She touched the screen and tried to stretch out the picture.

"That doesn't work on a flip phone," Leila said. "But look up there in the corner. What does that look like?"

Kait squinted some more, then she gasped. "Is that Big Dog?!"

MUSH

With new energy, Leila and Kait sprang off the bench and restarted their search for Big Dog. The thief wasn't hiding the costume—he was walking around in plain sight! It didn't take the girls long to find their target. "There!" Kait screeched.

Leila followed her finger across the stadium. "Where?"

"There! Next to the bleachers! I saw a big dog snout for a second, and then it disappeared into the crowd!"

"Let's go!" Leila and Kait bounded toward the left field bleachers.

Unfortunately, the puppies that had helped them make so much progress just a few minutes before were now slowing them down. When they finally got to the left field bleachers, Big Dog was nowhere to be found. "Has anyone seen the mascot?!" Kait yelled.

"Over there," someone pointed.

Leila looked up to see a big, floppy ear near the third-base dugout. "He's headed underground!" she said. The girls raced toward the tunnel as best they could through the crowd. "Excuse me," Leila said as she tried to politely push through. "Oh, sorry. Sorry, ma'am. Excuse me, sir. Can we just squeeze through here? Nugget, we don't have time for that!"

With Big Dog getting away, Kait pulled out one last trick. "Baxter! Mush!"

Baxter, who to this point had been half-heartedly waddling through the stadium, broke into a full gallop. Nugget's eyes lit up when he saw Baxter sprint ahead and joined him. Side-by-side, they looked like two tiny sled dogs. The crowd noticed and quickly parted to avoid getting bulldozed by the furry bullets.

"What did you do?!" Leila gasped as she struggled to catch up.

"It's a trick I taught him when I was little," Kait said, concentrating on holding the puppy under her arm like a football. "I thought he could pull me around on a sled."

The girls were closing in on their target. They just had one more corner to round. "Clear the way, everyone!" Kait yelled. "We're saving Big—OOOF!"

Someone stepped in her way just as she turned the corner. It was Jenny. Kait dropped the leash and almost dropped the puppy as she fell down.

"WHAT ARE YOU DOING?!" Kait yelled as she scrambled for the leash. "You're letting him get away!"

"Sorry, but you're wrong," Jenny said.

Before she could question Jenny, Leila caught a glimpse of the tunnel door closing. A mascot tail disappeared inside. "Quick!" she yelled as she let go of

Nugget's leash. "Before the door locks!" Nugget darted around fans, scampered between a hot dog vendor's legs and leaped over a small Yorkie in the aisle. He squeezed through the doorway just in time, and his leash even got stuck in the crack to keep the door from closing all the way.

"Let's go!" Leila yelled.

Kait picked herself up and got Baxter. "You're not gonna get away with this!" she shouted back to Jenny.

"I'm not getting away with anything! You're..."

The girls disappeared into the tunnel before Jenny could finish her sentence.

"There!" Leila said, pointing to a tall figure disappearing around the corner. She rescued Nugget and took off again. By this time, Baxter was pooped, so Kait scooped him underneath her other arm.

Carrying the two dogs, Kait was having a hard time walking, let alone jogging.

Nick stuck his head out of the mascot room when he heard the commotion. "What's going on?"

"We (gasp) found (gasp) Big Dog," Kait panted. "Take these." Kait and Leila dumped Baxter and the puppies at Nick's feet.

"Where?" he asked. "Down here?! I haven't seen him!"

Before Nick could get his answer, the girls and Nugget ran off again. The girls rounded the corner, then gasped. In the dim light, they could make out the silhouettes of not one, not two, but THREE Big Dogs jogging together at the end of the hallway! What?! Were they dealing with a gang of mascot thieves?!

Nugget led the girls in one final sprint to catch up before the Big Dogs rounded the third corner. But just as they started gaining ground, a head poked out of the security room. "No running through the halls!" Officer Franklin yelled.

The girls slowed to the fastest a person could shuffle without technically running. "We found Big Dog!" Leila said on her way by the security officer. "Actually we found three of them!"

Officer Franklin wrinkled her nose in disgust. "Three Big Dogs?! You girls need to stop this nonsense right now!"

"No can do!" Kait shouted as she shuffled faster. She turned to Leila. "Jenny and the police lady are both in on this too? How big is this gang?!" From up around the corner, the girls heard a big door open. Sunlight streamed into the hallway.

"Quick!" Leila shouted. "They're escaping!"

The girls skidded around the corner

and flew out the open door to find...

...Three giant hot dogs sprinting ahead.

Those weren't Big Dogs—they were big hot dogs, dressed up with dog tails, snouts and floppy ears to celebrate Bark at the Park. This was the sixth-inning hot dog race, not an elaborate mascot heist. Wait a second. If this was the hot dog race...

Leila looked up to find herself standing in the middle of left field with 10,000 pairs of eyes staring right back at her.

STADIUM JAIL

Stadium jail.

That's what Officer Franklin insisted on calling it. She explained that some professional stadiums have real jail cells with metal bars and everything to hold unruly fans, but the Middleburg Red Dogs only had this little room that they sometimes used for stadium jail and sometimes used for lost kids like Jenny Jones. "But make no mistake," Officer Franklin said right before she slammed the door on Leila, Kait and Nugget. "Right now, it's stadium jail."

Leila was on the verge of tears. She'd

hardly ever been in trouble before, let alone gotten thrown into jail. Kait, on the other hand, was defiant. "We'll fight this," Kait said. "We'll take it to the Supreme Court if we have to! This just burns me up. We were trying to do something good, and we make one little mistake..."

"Running onto the field is a big mistake," Leila corrected.

"...We make one ITTY, BITTY mistake," Kait continued, "And suddenly we're in jail? I don't think so! Not in America!"

Leila put her head in her hands. She had gotten so swept up in the hunt for the Big Dog that she'd stopped thinking. Why would there be three Big Dog costumes? That should have made her stop right there. And the sixth inning hot dog race was always her favorite part of the game. Hadn't she just been telling Kait about it?

After three unsuccessful laps around the room trying to find something to eat, Nugget jumped into Leila's lap and curled up. As Leila petted Nugget, she got her nerve back. "The only way we're escaping this without getting grounded for life is by solving the case. So let's look back at everything we know and try to figure it out."

"OK, let's start at the beginning," Kait said. "The first thing we know is that Jenny Jones is the worst."

"No! That's not something we know! All we know is that she brought a cat and a sign to a baseball game."

"And that she tackled me and tried to stop us from finding Big Dog," Kait said.

"Actually she was trying to keep us from getting thrown into stadium jail."

Kait rolled her eyes.

"And that's not even the beginning," Leila said. "The beginning is when Mrs. Gilmore gave Nick the costume."

"Do you think Mrs. Gilmore stole her own costume so she could fire Nick?" Kait asked. "She doesn't seem to like him very much."

"She liked him just fine until he ruined the costume," Leila said. "I don't think she stole it."

"Well then maybe Nick?"

"Maybe, but I don't know why. Wouldn't he want to wait until after the game to steal the costume?"

Kait spun her chair around and sat in it backward because that seemed like something a police detective would do. "I'll tell you who I think it was," Kait said. "I think it was the security lady."

Leila thought about it for a second.

She was the only one in the room when the costume went missing. "Maybe," she finally said. "But why?"

"Because we were trying to solve a crime, and that's her job! This is what she wanted all along. She was scared because we're so much better than her at her job."

"You're saying she knew we were coming to the game, so she figured out a way to lock us up so we wouldn't take her job one day?"

"The perfect crime," Kait said, looking off into the distance like she'd just solved the biggest case of her life.

Leila shook her head. "We're missing something."

Just then the door opened. Nick walked in with Baxter and Mrs. Gilmore. "You two waiting for your parents?" Nick asked.

"Stadium jail," Kait replied matter-of-factly.

"There's no such thing as 'stadium jail,'" Mrs. Gilmore replied with squinty eyes.

"But that lady said..." Kait stopped when she saw Officer Franklin walk through the door with Leila's dad.

"You told them they were in stadium jail?" Mrs. Gilmore asked Officer Franklin.

"That's right," she said. "And I brought the judge."

Leila's dad shook his head. "Leila, how could you..."

"I'm so sorry, Dad! The hot dog was dressed up like a real dog!"

Mr. Beal looked more confused than ever. "You'll have to explain in the car. Let's go."

Leila hung her head. She really wasn't going to solve this case. "OK."

Nick stepped up. "I'm sorry about all this," he said to Leila. "I really appreciate you trying to help me, even though you're gonna get in trouble for it."

"And I'm sorry about not solving your mystery," Leila said. "I tried my best." Nugget looked sad about not finding Big

Dog too.

Nick petted Nugget. "It's OK," he said. "You guys did great." He handed Baxter over to Kait. "Your dog really liked hanging out with the puppies. He couldn't stop licking them!"

Leila's head snapped up. "What did you say?"

"It was really funny," Nick said. "He kept licking and licking."

"But Baxter doesn't like other dogs. Especially puppies."

Nick shrugged. "Well, he liked these ones. He liked them so much that he was even licking their blanket!"

Leila's eyes got wide. "I solved it!" she said.

Officer Franklin rolled her eyes. "Not again."

"No, for real! I solved it, I solved it, I solved it!"

"Solved what?" Mrs. Gilmore asked. "You know who took the costume?"

Leila nodded and pointed at Officer Franklin. "Her!"

DOG OF THE YEAR

"WHAT?!" Officer Franklin bellowed. Mrs. Gilmore looked up in surprise. Officer Franklin started walking toward Leila with her finger pointed at Leila's chest. "YOUNG LADY, YOU'D BETTER..."

"Wait, no no no. It's not bad! You didn't do it on purpose!"

"WHAT DO YOU MEAN I DIDN'T DO IT ON PURPOSE?! I'M THE SECURITY OFFICER! I THINK I'D KNOW IF I WERE STEALING SOMETHING! I WISH WE DID HAVE A STADIUM JAIL BECAUSE I

WOULD..."

"Can I just show you what I mean," Leila suggested. "I think it would be a lot easier if I showed you all."

Mrs. Gilmore sighed. "As long as it's not on the field."

Leila nodded and led the way back to the mascot room. As she did, she started her explanation. "I thought it was weird earlier that Nugget was licking the puppies so much. He loves other dogs, but he usually plays with them, not licks them."

As if to prove Leila's point, Nugget tried climbing onto Baxter's back as the two dogs walked down the hallway. Baxter stopped and grumbled.

Leila pointed to the two dogs and continued. "As weird as it was for Nugget to lick the puppies, it was downright crazy for Baxter to do that. He hates other dogs."

Kait jumped in. "He doesn't hate them, but he does like his Baxter time."

"You still haven't explained your brilliant idea of why dogs licking other dogs means I stole a costume," Officer Franklin said.

Just then, the group walked into the mascot room. Leila stopped. "It's pretty cold in here."

"It has to be," Mrs. Gilmore said. "There's no sweating in the Big Dog costume."

"That's true, but it's probably too cold for puppies."

"Way too cold for puppies!" Officer Franklin said. "You have to realize they don't wear clothes like you. And they're not big balls of fur yet like these dogs."

Nugget and Baxter looked at each other.

"So you helped, right officer?" Leila said.

"Of course I helped! I wrapped the puppies in a blanket because Rick over here forgot," she said, gesturing to Nick.

"And where did you find the blanket?"

"I don't know, it was lying somewhere in the room."

Leila smiled and started moving the puppies off their blanket. "It was draped over the chair," she said. With that, she flung open the blanket. Everyone in the room gasped. Scrunched up in a ball, it looked like a nice, soft puppy blanket. But spread out like this, everyone could see the "blanket" actually had two arms and two legs. It could only be one thing.

"BIG DOG!" Kait exclaimed.

Officer Franklin's eyes got wide. "I had no idea," she said.

"It's OK!" Leila said. "You were just trying to help! And it's white and furry inside, just like a blanket."

"Except for the big, red stain in the middle," Mrs. Gilmore said.

"Thank goodness for that stain!" Leila said. "That's what solved the case. See, Nugget doesn't usually lick other dogs, but he does love sweets."

"Like Juicy Red!" Kait exclaimed.

Leila nodded. "With the dogs licking both the puppies and the blanket, I knew something had to be up. That's when I remembered the Juicy Red."

Mrs. Gilmore picked up the costume and slowly shook her head with a smile on her face. "You girls did it! My husband's going to be so happy! What can I do to repay you? We can give you season tickets!"

Leila looked at Kait, who was making

a throw-up face at the thought of having to go to a whole season's worth of baseball games. Then Leila looked back at Mrs. Gilmore. "Actually, we thought maybe you could do something for someone else." She nodded at Nick.

"Mrs. Gilmore," Nick said. "I'm sorry for ruining your husband's costume. It's a great costume, and I should have been more careful with it. Also, um, I did find something that should take out the stain. Do you think I could try it?"

Mrs. Gilmore looked unsure. "Please, can you let him give it a try?" Leila asked. "I think it'll work." Mrs. Gilmore sighed and handed over the costume.

"Thank you!" Nick pulled baking soda out of his pocket and turned to Leila. "Did you get what I asked?"

Leila nodded and handed over the vinegar packets. Mrs. Gilmore looked nervous as Nick mixed the vinegar and baking soda together into a paste and rubbed it into the stain. Everyone gathered around. Nick looked at his phone for the next instructions. "Now, we're supposed to rinse it off and see what happens."

Nick rinsed the stain with bottled water while everyone else held their breaths. After he rinsed and wiped the stain, Mrs. Gilmore leaned in. "Whoa!" she said. "That's incredible!"

Nick could breathe again. The stain was gone. While Nick finished wiping, Mrs. Gilmore turned to Leila and Kait. "You girls truly are incredible! There must be something I can do to thank you for all you've done today!"

"Well," Leila said, looking at Nugget. "There is one more thing."

Forty-five minutes later, Nugget

happily jogged onto the field. But this time, the crowd was cheering, not gasping. After the game finished, Nugget and 200 other dogs finally got to march around the bases for the Pup Parade. Marching on Nugget's right was his new girlfriend, Penelope the cavapoo. On his left, looking happier than he'd looked all day, was Baxter. "See Baxter, this isn't so bad," Kait said, pushing the tired dog on a cart Mrs. Gilmore had dug out of a supply closet.

As she rounded first base, Leila grinned at all the familiar faces in the parade. There was the Great Dane and the Chihuahua. Mrs. Gilmore had taken a break from worrying about everything to show off her puppies. Jenny Jones had even joined the parade, proudly holding her cat. And leading everyone, practically dancing around the bases, was Nick in the Big Dog costume.

After the parade, Mrs. Gilmore stepped to a podium in front of home plate. "Every year, we crown one dog as the Middleburg Dog of the Year. Well, this year, as you might have noticed, is a little different. We wouldn't even have had Pup Parade this year if it weren't for two very special dogs. That's why—for the first time ever—we have a tie for Dog of the Year. Ladies and gentlemen, I'd like to introduce you to your Middleburg Dogs of the Year: Nugget and Baxter!"

AUTHORS' NOTE

Hope you had as much fun reading Leila and Nugget's adventures as we did writing them! If you liked these books, would you consider telling a friend or posting a short review on Amazon? We'd really appreciate the help!

Also, we'd love to hear from you! You can email us about anything at dustin@dustinbradybooks.com.

Thanks again for reading our books!

ABOUT THE AUTHORS

Deserae and Dustin Brady are the parents of Leila Brady (a baby) and Nugget Brady (a dog). They live in Cleveland, Ohio.

ABOUT THE ILLUSTRATOR

April Brady is a professional illustrator in Pensacola, Florida. Deserae and Dustin feel lucky to have such a talented doggy-drawer as a sister-in-law.

Lightning Source UK Ltd.
Milton Keynes UK
UKHW02f1824300518
323481UK00030B/506/P